PUFFIN BOOKS

THE PUFFIN BOOK OF NURSERY RHYMES

For centuries each generation has been linked to the next by the shared laughter of nursery rhymes; and it has been said that one of the best investments a family can make is a good nursery rhyme book.

Here is a notable collection of nursery rhymes, for it is a fresh gathering from the memories of grandmothers and the byways of folk literature. As well as containing all the familiar jingles it introduces a number of traditional rhymes which have hitherto been known only locally or in individual families. In fact, this is a sparkling treasury of memorable verses, as lovingly planned as a poetry anthology; it is also annotated, and it is indexed both by subject and by first lines. To complete the pleasure, the book is illustrated on almost every page with exquisite pictures by Pauline Baynes.

This is the first comprehensive collection of nursery rhymes to be produced as a paperback, and it has been specially prepared by two of the foremost authorities on children's lore. In 1964 it won the International Prize of the City of Caorle.

The Puffin Book of

Nursery Rhymes

gathered by Iona and Peter Opie

With illustrations by Pauline Baynes

Puffin Books

Puffin Books, Penguin Books Ltd, Harmondsworth, Middlesex, England
Penguin Books, 40 West 23rd Street, New York, New York 10010, U.S.A.
Penguin Books Australia Ltd, Ringwood, Victoria, Australia
Penguin Books Canada Ltd, 2801 John Street Markham, Ontario, Canada L3R 1B4
Penguin Books (N.Z.) Ltd, 182–190 Wairau Road, Auckland 10, New Zealand

—

First published 1963
Reprinted 1964, 1966, 1968, 1970 (twice), 1971, 1972, 1974, 1975 (twice),
1976, 1977, 1978, 1979, 1980, 1982, 1983

—

—

Made and printed in Great Britain
by Richard Clay (The Chaucer Press) Ltd,
Bungay, Suffolk
Set in Monotype Bembo

Contents

Preface

'OLD friends are best,' King James exclaimed, as he called for the old shoes that easiest fitted his feet. And a book of nursery rhymes is a book of old friends indeed. Yet it has long been observed that 'familiaritie breedythe contempt'. The poet's children, who see the great man each morning blowing upon his porridge, are seldom likely to read his poetry. In this anthology it is our purpose, as in our previous nursery rhyme books, to try to reconcile these two sayings. If this book, inevitably, is a gathering of the most familiar verses of our infancy, it may yet be possible to show that the nursery estate is more happily endowed than is sometimes supposed.

Oral rhymes are the true waifs of our literature in that their original wordings, as well as their authors, are usually unknown. But this does not mean that they are necessarily sickly strays to whom only an indulgent and undiscriminating nursery will give shelter. Rather it is true that having to fend for themselves, without the benefit of sponsor or sheepskin binding, they have had to be wonderfully fit to have survived. If Auden and Garrett's definition of poetry, that it is 'memorable speech', contains no more than a tincture of truth, it is yet enough to dye the rhymes with the tints of poetry. They owe their present existence to this one quality of memorability.

It is typical of the perverse workings of oral tradition that few of the nursery rhymes should have originally been intended for the young. In *The Oxford Dictionary of Nursery Rhymes* we show how many of them are unrelated snatches of worldly songs, adult jests, lampoons, proverbial maxims, charms, and country ballads. The mother or nurse of former days did not croon her ditties because they were songs for children, but because – with her sleeves rolled up and arms in the wash-tub – they were the first verses to come into her mind when the children had to be amused.

7

And since she might be singing a popular song of her own day, as readily as one that was sung by her forbears, we find that the dates of the rhymes are fascinatingly various. While some were already ancient lore when Shakespeare was a boy, others are but second or third hand memories of songs first heard in Victorian music halls. Thus in a representative collection of nursery rhymes we have preserved for us, by what amounts to communal consent, an anthology of the most memorable verses from each of the centuries of our history. And if the test of a poet is 'the frequency and diversity of the occasions on which we remember his poetry', then Mother Goose deserves a monument in Westminster Abbey, and a good nursery rhyme book should be every poet's primer.

In this fresh gathering of nursery rhymes we have ventured to arrange the verses as a poetry anthology. Instead of accentuating their oddness and variety by mixing them up, as is general in nursery rhyme books, we have attempted at each opening of pages to bring like with like; we have emphasized (and even indexed) their subject matter; and we have endeavoured, as much as possible, so to order the rhymes on a page that the reader may pass easily from one to the next without feeling it necessary to take a deep breath in between. In our choice of rhymes, too, we have had the advantage of being able to draw upon the results of nearly twenty years' collecting, and this has enabled us to choose the rhyme or version of a rhyme which seemed to us to sound best or mean most when set with its neighbours.

In the back of the memory of each one of us there is a store of rhymes, perhaps as many as a hundred and fifty, which we 'know', if only we could remember them; and it is the first duty of any nursery rhyme book to provide these texts on request. Having done this, the anthologist can have the pleasure of making introductions; and it is perhaps a measure of the wealth of English traditional verse that while *The Oxford Nursery Rhyme Book*, with its 800 rhymes, stands as the chief collection (it is designed to be a family book), every rhyme in the present collection, after supplying the 150 standard rhymes, is either additional to those in the Oxford book or a distinctly different version. In other words there are over two hundred introductions, and the possessor of both books will have 1,000 rhymes at his fingertips – if not in his head.

For permission to make use here of this repository of traditional verse we are indebted to the University Press, Oxford (The Clarendon Press), for whom we started and are still collecting. That we possess this archive to draw upon we owe in part to the always welcome contributions which we have received from correspondents, now more than a thousand in all parts of the English-speaking world, each of whom has seemed to be blessed with such memory and humour that we have come to feel that these two virtues must be related. A number of industrious persons, too, have collected for us over the years, and this book owes particular debts of gratitude to Miss Joan Ford (Alton); Miss F. Doreen Gullen (Scarborough); Mr H. W. Harwood (Halifax); Miss Carrol Jenkins (Bath); Miss B. A. Kneller (Nutfield); Miss Joyce A. Terrett (Swansea); Miss Ruth L. Tongue (Crowcombe); and Mr S. B. Vickers (Market Rasen); as also to Mrs Gillian Davies, who has given her time to assembling the material 'on the site'. The names of a few other contributors of special rhymes and songs traditional in their families, and here printed for the first time, will be found in the notes.

It will be seen that in this collection, as also in the notes at the end of the book, we are considering nursery rhymes as literature or, at least, as reading-matter. We would suggest that there are few books more attractive to a small child who wants to learn to read than a nursery rhyme book. He already knows a number of rhymes or parts of them, and he can gain confidence by pretending to read what he already knows. The illustrations guide him to the subject-matter, and when he has to guess a word the rhythm and rhyme are sometimes a powerful assistance. Since, too, we have grouped together rhymes about the same subjects, such as dogs, cats, astronauts, and apple pies, the veriest beginner can learn to identify the repetition of a key word on a page, and so, perhaps, almost unconsciously become friends with 'printed language'. Further, this book is a paperback and expendable. It does not matter if a child handles and manhandles it, if he colours a page with paint or jam, or if he falls asleep on it in his bed. It is, in fact, the modern equivalent of the pedlar's chapbook of the eighteenth and early nineteenth century, in whose paper covers many of the nursery rhymes found their first printed home. And even though there will be much that he cannot immediately understand (for may he not think, and rightly, that this is really a grown-up book?), he will possess it as his own, secure in the knowledge that it can, with his parents' skill, be made to sing the songs he knows and loves.

West Liss, Hampshire   I.O. & P.O.

We wish you health,
We wish you wealth,
We wish you gold in store,
We wish you may enjoy this book,
What could we wish you more?

An Apple Pie

A   was an Apple Pie

B   Bit it

C   Cut it

D   Dealt it

E   Eat it

F   Fought for it

G   Got it

H   Had it

I   Inspected it

J   Jumped for it

K   Kept it

L   Longed for it

M   Mourned for it

N   Nodded at it

O   Opened it

P Peeped in it

Q Quartered it

R Ran for it

S Stole it

T Took it

U Upset it

V Viewed it

W Wanted it

X, Y, Z and ampersand
All wished for a piece in hand

Who made the pie?
I did.
Who stole the pie?
He did.
Who found the pie?
She did.
Who ate the pie?
You did.
Who cried for pie?
We all did.

Apple pie, pudding, and pancakes,
All begins with A.

Hey Diddle Diddle

Hey diddle diddle,
  The cat and the fiddle,
The cow jumped over the moon;
  The little dog laughed
  To see such sport,
And the dish ran away with the spoon.

Puss came dancing out of the barn
With a pair of bagpipes under her arm;
She could play nothing but 'Fiddle cum fee,
The fly hath married the bumble bee'.
Then all the birds of the air did sing,
'Did ever you hear so merry a thing?'
Fiddle cum fee, fiddle cum fee,
The fly hath married the bumble bee!

Rub-a-dub-dub

Rub-a-dub-dub,
Three men in a tub,
And who do you think they be?
The butcher, the baker,
The candlestick-maker,
Turn 'em out, knaves all three.

Three wise men of Gotham
Went to sea in a bowl,
If the bowl had been stronger
My song had been longer.

Little Boys

What are little boys made of?
Frogs and snails
And puppy-dogs' tails
That's what little boys are made of.

Georgie Porgie, pudding and pie,
Kissed the girls and made them cry;
When the boys came out to play,
Georgie Porgie ran away.

Andy Pandy, fine and dandy,
Loves plum cake and sugar candy.
Bought it from a candy shop
And away did hop, hop, hop.

Ginger, Ginger, broke the winder,
Hit the winder – Crack!
The baker came out to give 'im a clout
And landed on 'is back.

Tom, Tom, the piper's son,
Stole a pig and away he run;
The pig was eat, and Tom was beat,
And Tom went howling down the street.

Diddle diddle dumpling, my son John,
Went to bed with his trousers on;
One shoe off, and the other shoe on,
Diddle diddle dumpling, my son John.

Jeremiah Obadiah, puff, puff, puff.
When he gives his messages he snuffs, snuffs, snuffs,
When he goes to school by day, he roars, roars, roars,
When he goes to bed at night he snores, snores, snores,
When he goes to Christmas treat he eats plum-duff,
Jeremiah Obadiah, puff, puff, puff.

17

Little Girls

What are little girls made of?
  Sugar and spice
  And all things nice
That's what little girls are made of.

There was a little girl, and she had a little curl
  Right in the middle of her forehead;
When she was good she was very, very good,
  But when she was bad she was horrid.

She stood on her head, on her little truckle-bed,
  With nobody by for to hinder;
She screamed and she squalled, she yelled and she bawled,
  And drummed her little heels against the winder.

Her mother heard the noise and thought it was the boys,
  A-kicking up a rumpus in the attic;
But when she climbed the stair, and saw Jemima there,
  She took her and did whip her most emphatic.

Lucy Locket lost her pocket,
Kitty Fisher found it;
Not a penny was there in it,
Only ribbon round it.

Round and round the butter dish,
 One, two, three,
If you want a pretty girl
 Just pick me.

See-saw, Margery Daw,
Sold her bed and lay upon straw,
Sold the straw and lay upon grass
To buy herself a looking-glass.

Little Betty Blue
 Lost her holiday shoe,
What can little Betty do?
 Give her another
 To match the other,
And then she may walk out in two.

Here's Sulky Sue,
What shall we do?
Turn her face to the wall
Till she comes to.

Ten Little Pussy Cats

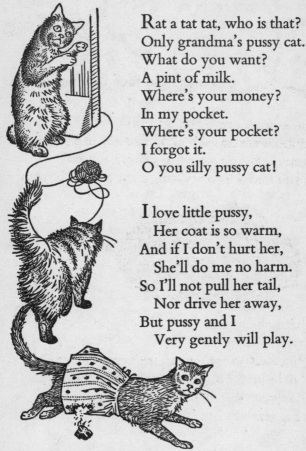

Rat a tat tat, who is that?
Only grandma's pussy cat.
What do you want?
A pint of milk.
Where's your money?
In my pocket.
Where's your pocket?
I forgot it.
O you silly pussy cat!

I love little pussy,
    Her coat is so warm,
And if I don't hurt her,
    She'll do me no harm.
So I'll not pull her tail,
    Nor drive her away,
But pussy and I
    Very gently will play.

Pussy cat mew jumped over a coal,
And in her best petticoat burnt a great hole;
Pussy cat mew shall have no more milk,
Till her best petticoat's mended with silk.

Five little pussy cats sitting in a row,
Blue ribbons round each neck, fastened in a bow.
Hey pussies! Ho pussies! Are your faces clean?
Don't you know you're sitting there so as to be seen?

Pussy cat, pussy cat, where have you been?
I've been to London to look at the queen.
Pussy cat, pussy cat, what did you there?
I frightened a little mouse under her chair.

Pussicat, wussicat, with a white foot,
When is your wedding, and I'll come to it.
The beer's to brew, the bread's to bake,
Pussicat, wussicat, don't be too late.

One for the Pot

There was a little man,
And he had a little gun,
And his bullets were made of lead, lead, lead;
He went to the brook
And shot a little duck,
Right through the middle of the head, head, head.

He carried it home
To his old wife Joan,
And bade her a fire for to make, make, make,
To roast the little duck
He had shot in the brook,
And he'd go and fetch her the drake, drake, drake.

The drake was a-swimming
With his little curly tail,
When the little man made it his mark, mark, mark;
He let off his gun,
But he fired too soon,
And the drake flew away with a quack, quack, quack.

Jack, Jack Joe,
Bent his bow,
Shot at a pigeon
And killed a crow.

The House that Jack Built

This is the 🏠 that Jack built.

This is the 🛍️ that lay in the 🏠 that Jack built.

This is the 🐀 that ate the 🛍️ that lay in the 🏠 that Jack built.

This is the 🐈 that killed the 🐀 that ate the 🛍️ that lay in the 🏠 that Jack built.

This is the 🐕 that worried the 🐈 that killed the 🐀 that ate the 🛍️ that lay in the 🏠 that Jack built.

This is the 🐄 with the crumpled horn that tossed the 🐕 that worried the 🐈 that killed the 🐀 that ate the 🛍️ that lay in the 🏠 that Jack built.

This is the 🖼 all forlorn that milked the 🖼 with the crumpled horn that tossed the 🖼 that worried the 🖼 that killed the 🖼 that ate the 🖼 that lay in the 🖼 that Jack built.

This is the 🖼 all tattered and torn that kissed the 🖼 all forlorn that milked the 🖼 with the crumpled horn that tossed the 🖼 that worried the 🖼 that killed the 🖼 that ate the 🖼 that lay in the 🖼 that Jack built.

This is the 🖼 all shaven and shorn that married the 🖼 all tattered and torn that kissed the 🖼 all forlorn that milked the 🖼 with the crumpled horn that tossed the 🖼 that worried the 🖼 that killed the 🖼 that ate the 🖼 that lay in the 🖼 that Jack built.

This is the  that crowed in the morn that waked the 🧑 all shaven and shorn that married the 🧑 all tattered and torn that kissed the 👤 all forlorn that milked the 🐄 with the crumpled horn that tossed the 🐕 that worried the 🐈 that killed the 🐀 that ate the 🌾 that lay in the 🏠 that Jack built.

This is the 🧑 sowing his corn that kept the 🐓 that crowed in the morn that waked the 🧑 all shaven and shorn that married the 🧑 all tattered and torn that kissed the 👤 all forlorn that milked the 🐄 with the crumpled horn that tossed the 🐕 that worried the 🐈 that killed the 🐀 that ate the 🌾 that lay in the 🏠 that Jack built.

A Herd of Little Cows

I had a little cow,
Hey-diddle, ho-diddle!
I had a little cow, and it had a little calf;
Hey-diddle, ho-diddle! and there's my song half.

I had a little cow,
Hey-diddle, ho-diddle!
I had a little cow, and I drove it to the stall;
Hey-diddle, ho-diddle! and there's my song all.

I had a little cow and to save her,
I turned her into the meadow to graze her;
There came a heavy storm of rain,
And drove the little cow home again.
The church doors they stood open,
And there the little cow was cropen;
The bell-ropes they were made of hay,
And the little cow ate them all away;
The sexton came to toll the bell,
And pushed the little cow into the well!

Cushy cow, bonny, let down thy milk,
And I will give thee a gown of silk;
A gown of silk and a silver tee,
If thou wilt let down thy milk to me.

Four stiff-standers,
Four dilly-danders,
Two lookers, two crookers,
And a wig-wag.

There was a little man and he had a little cow,
    And he had no fodder to give her,
So he took up his fiddle and played her this tune,
    'Consider, good cow, consider,
This isn't the time for the grass to grow,
    Consider, good cow, consider.'
So the poor little cow lay down on her side,
And considered, and considered, and considered,
    till she died.

Old Roger is dead and laid in his grave,
　Laid in his grave, laid in his grave;
Old Roger is dead and laid in his grave,
　H'm ha! laid in his grave.

They planted an apple tree over his head,
　Over his head, over his head;
They planted an apple tree over his head,
　H'm ha! over his head.

The apples grew ripe and ready to fall,
　Ready to fall, ready to fall;
The apples grew ripe and ready to fall,
　H'm ha! ready to fall.

There came an old woman a-picking them all,
　A-picking them all, a-picking them all;
There came an old woman a-picking them all,
　H'm ha! picking them all.

Old Roger jumps up and gives her a knock,
　Gives her a knock, gives her a knock;
Which makes the old woman go hipperty-hop,
　H'm ha! hipperty-hop.

Good Apple Tree

Here's to thee, good apple tree,
Stand fast at root,
Bear well at top,
Every little twig
Bear an apple big,
Every little bough
Bear apples enow,
Hats full! Caps full!
Three score sacks full!
Hurrah, boys! Hurrah!

Up in the green orchard there is a green tree,
The finest of pippins that you may see;
The apples are ripe, and ready to fall,
And Robin and Richard shall gather them all.

As I went up the apple tree
All the apples fell on me;
Bake a pudding, bake a pie,
Send it up to John MacKay;
John MacKay is not in,
Send it up to the man in the moon.

On the Farm

Baa, baa, black sheep,
　　Have you any wool?
Yes, sir, yes, sir,
　　Three bags full;
One for the master,
　　And one for the dame,
And one for the little boy
　　Who lives down the lane.

When the white pinks begin to appear,
This is the time your sheep to shear.

My maid Mary
　　She minds her dairy,
While I go a-hoeing and mowing each morn;
　　Merrily run the reel,
　　And the little spinning-wheel,
Whilst I am singing and mowing my corn.

Lazy Farm Boys

Little Boy Blue come blow your horn,
The sheep's in the meadow, the cow's in the corn.
Where is the boy that looks after the sheep?
He's under a haycock fast asleep.
Will you wake him? No, not I!
For if I do, he's sure to cry.

Pick, crow, pick, and have no fear,
I sit here and I don't care.
If my master chance to come,
You must fly and I must run.

He that would thrive
Must rise at five;
He that hath thriven
May lie till seven;
And he that by the plough would thrive,
Himself must either hold or drive.

Horsemanship

How go the ladies, how go they?
　Amble, amble, all the way.
How go lords and gentlemen?
　Trit, trot, trit, and home again.
How goes the farmer, how goes he?
　Hobble-de-gee, hobble-de-gee.
How goes the butcher boy who longs to be rich?
　A-gallop, a-gallop, a-gallop,
　　– A-plonk in the ditch!

I had a little pony
　His name was Dapple Gray;
I lent him to a lady
　To ride a mile away.
She whipped him, she slashed him,
　She rode him through the mire;
I would not lend my pony now,
　For all the lady's hire.

BUYING A HORSE

One white foot, buy him,
Two white feet, try him,
Three white feet, look well about him,
Four white feet, do without him.

RULES WHEN RIDING

Your head and your heart keep up,
Your hands and your heels keep down,
Your knees keep close to your horse's side,
And your elbows close to your own.

THE HORSE'S PETITION

Up a hill hurry me not,
Down a hill flurry me not,
When I'm hot, water me not,
In the stable forget me not.

The Cuckoo

Sunshine and rain
Brings the cuckoo from Spain;
The first cock of hay
Frights the cuckoo away.

The cuckoo comes in April,
Sings a song in May,
In the middle of June another tune,
And then he flies away.

The cuckoo is a merry bird,
   She sings as she flies;
She brings us good tidings,
   And tells us no lies.
She sippeth sweet flowers
   To keep her voice clear,
That she may sing Cuckoo!
   Three months in the year.

The Owl

There was an owl lived in an oak,
The more he heard, the less he spoke,
The less he spoke, the more he heard –
O if men were all like that wise bird.

Of all the gay birds that e'er I did see,
The owl is the fairest by far to me,
For all day long she sits in a tree,
And when the night comes away flies she.

There was an owl lived in an oak,
   Wisky, wasky, weedle;
And every word he ever spoke
   Was, Fiddle, faddle, feedle.
A gunner chanced to come that way,
   Wisky, wasky, weedle;
Says he, I'll shoot you, silly bird,
   Fiddle, faddle, feedle.

The Happy Courtship,
Merry Marriage, and Picnic Dinner of

Cock Robin and Jenny Wren

It was on a merry time,
  When Jenny Wren was young,
So neatly as she danced,
  And so sweetly as she sung.

Robin Redbreast lost his heart,
  He was a gallant bird;
He doffed his hat to Jenny,
  And thus to her he said:

'My dearest Jenny Wren,
  If you will but be mine,
You shall dine on cherry pie,
  And drink nice currant wine.

'I'll dress you like a goldfinch,
  Or like a peacock gay;
So, if you'll have me, Jenny,
  Let us appoint the day.'

Jenny blushed behind her fan,
  And thus declared her mind:
'Then let it be tomorrow, Bob,
  I take your offer kind.

'Cherry pie is very good,
    So is currant wine;
But I will wear my russet gown
    And never dress too fine.'

Robin rose up early,
    At the break of day,
He flew to Jenny Wren's house
    To sing a roundelay.

He met the Cock and Hen,
    And bade the Cock declare
This would be his wedding day,
    With Jenny Wren the fair.

The Cock then blew his horn,
    To let the neighbours know,
This was Robin's wedding day,
    And they might see the show.

The first that came was Parson Rook,
    With spectacles and band;
A bible and a prayer book
    He held within his hand.

Then followed him the Lark,
    For he could sweetly sing,
And he was to be clerk
    At Cock Robin's wedding.

He sang of Robin's love
    For little Jenny Wren;
And when he came unto the end,
    Then he began again.

Then came the bride and bridegroom;
    Quite plainly was she dressed,
And blushed so much, her cheeks they were
    As red as Robin's breast.

But Robin cheered her up;
    'My pretty Jen,' said he,
'We're going to be married,
    And contented we shall be.'

The Goldfinch came on next,
    To give away the bride;
The Linnet, being bridesmaid,
    Walked by Jenny's side.

And as she was a-walking,
    Said, 'Upon my word,
I think that your Cock Robin
    Is a very pretty bird.'

'Now then,' says Parson Rook,
  'Who gives this maid away?'
'I do,' responds the Goldfinch,
  'And her dowry I will pay.

'Here's a kettle and a cooking pot,
  And other things beside;
Now happy be the bridegroom,
  And happy be the bride.'

'And will you have her, Robin,
  To be your wedded wife?'
'Yes, I will,' says Robin,
  'And love her all my life.'

'And will you have him, Jenny,
  Your husband now to be?'
'Yes, I will,' says Jenny,
  'And love him heartily.'

Then on her slender finger
    Cock Robin put the ring;
'You're married now,' says Parson Rook,
    While loud the lark did sing:

'Happy be the bridegroom,
    And happy be the bride;
And may not man, nor bird, nor beast,
    This happy pair divide.'

The birds were asked to dine;
    Not Jenny's friends alone,
But every pretty songster
    That had Cock Robin known.

They supped on cherry pie,
    Besides some currant wine,
And every guest brought something,
    That sumptuous they might dine.

They each took up a bumper
    To toast the loving pair:
Cock Robin the proud bridegroom,
    And Jenny Wren the fair.

Royal Economy

When good King Arthur ruled this land,
   He was a goodly king;
He stole three pecks of barley-meal
   To make a bag-pudding.

A bag-pudding the king did make,
   And stuffed it well with plums;
And in it put great lumps of fat,
   As big as my two thumbs.

The king and queen did eat thereof,
   And noblemen beside;
And what they could not eat that night,
   The queen next morning fried.

Queen, Queen Caroline,
Washed her hair in turpentine,
Turpentine to make it shine,
Queen, Queen Caroline.

Whence and Whither

Pretty maid, pretty maid,
   Where have you been?
Gathering a posy
   To give to the Queen.
Pretty maid, pretty maid,
   What gave she you?
She gave me a diamond
   As big as my shoe.

Little maid, little maid, where have you been?
I've been to see grandmother over the green.
What did she give you? Milk in a can.
What did you say for it? Thank you, Grandam.

Milkman, milkman, where have you been?
In Buttermilk Channel up to my chin;
I spilt my milk, and I spoilt my clothes,
And got a long icicle hung from my nose.

Willy boy, Willy boy, where are you going?
    I will go with you if that I may.
I'm going to the meadow to see them a-mowing,
    I am going to help them to make the new hay.

Little maid, pretty maid, whither goest thou?
Down to the meadow to milk my cow.
Shall I go with thee? No, not now;
When I send for thee, then come thou.

Little boy, little boy, where were you born?
Up in the Highlands among the green corn.
Little boy, little boy, where did you sleep?
In the byre with the kye, in the cot with the sheep.

Dreams and Ambitions

The fair maid who, the First of May,
　Goes to the fields at break of day,
And washes in dew from the hawthorn tree,
　Will ever after handsome be.

A Friday night's dream on a Saturday told,
Is sure to come true be it ever so old.

Bonny lass, canny lass,
　If thou wilt be mine,
Thou shalt not wash dishes
　Nor yet feed the swine,
Thou shalt sit on a cushion
　And sew a fine seam,
And feed upon strawberries,
　Sugar and cream.

When I was a little boy
  My mammy kept me in,
But now I am a great boy
  I'm fit to serve the king;
I can hand a musket,
  And I can smoke a pipe,
And I can kiss a pretty girl
  At twelve o'clock at night.

Lavender's blue, diddle, diddle,
  Lavender's green,
When I am king, diddle, diddle,
  You shall be queen.

Call up your men, diddle, diddle,
  Set them to work,
Some to the plough, diddle, diddle,
  Some to the cart.

Some to make hay, diddle, diddle,
  Some to thresh corn,
Whilst you and I, diddle, diddle,
  Keep ourselves warm.

Merry are the Bells

Merry are the bells, and merry would they ring,
Merry was myself, and merry could I sing;
With a merry ding-dong, happy, gay, and free,
And a merry sing-song, happy let us be.

THE BELLS OF LONDON

Oranges and lemons,
Say the bells of St Clement's.
You owe me five farthings,
Say the bells of St Martin's.
When will you pay me?
Say the bells of Old Bailey.
When I grow rich,
Say the bells of Shoreditch.
When will that be?
Say the bells of Stepney.
I'm sure I don't know,
Says the Great Bell of Bow.

46

A nut and a kernel,
Say the bells of Acton Burnell.
A pudding in the pot,
Say the bells of Acton Scott.
Pitch 'em and patch 'em,
Say the bells of Old Atcham.
Under and over,
Say the bells of Condover.
An old lump of wood,
Say the bells of Leebotwood.
Three crows on a tree,
Say the bells of Oswestry.
Buttermilk and whey,
Say the bells of Hopesay.
Roast beef and be merry,
Say the bells of Shrewsbury.
A new-born baby,
Say the bells of St Mary.

THE BELLS OF NORTHAMPTON

Roast beef and marshmallows,
Say the bells of All Hallows'.
Pancakes and fritters,
Say the bells of St Peter's.
Roast beef and boil'd,
Say the bells of St Giles'.
Poker and tongs,
Say the bells of St John's.

See-saw, Jack in the hedge,
Which is the way to London Bridge?
Put on your shoes, and away you trudge,
That is the way to London Bridge.

See-saw, sacradown,
Which is the way to London town?
One foot up and the other foot down,
That is the way to London town.
And just the same, over dale and hill,
Is also the way to wherever you will.

How many miles to Babylon?
Three score miles and ten.
Can I get there by candle-light?
Yes, and back again.
If your heels are nimble and light,
You may get there by candle-light.

London Bridge is Broken Down

London Bridge is broken down,
    Dance over the Lady Lea;
London Bridge is broken down,
    With a gay lady.

Then we must build it up again,
    Dance over the Lady Lea;
Then we must build it up again,
    With a gay lady.

What shall we build it up withal?
    Dance over the Lady Lea;
What shall we build it up withal?
    With a gay lady.

Build it up with iron and steel,
    Dance over the Lady Lea;
Build it up with iron and steel,
    With a gay lady.

Iron and steel will bend and break,
  Dance over the Lady Lea;
Iron and steel will bend and break,
  With a gay lady.

Build it up with wood and stone,
  Dance over the Lady Lea;
Build it up with wood and stone,
  With a gay lady.

Wood and stone will fall away,
  Dance over the Lady Lea;
Wood and stone will fall away,
  With a gay lady.

Build it up with silver and gold,
  Dance over the Lady Lea;
Build it up with silver and gold,
  With a gay lady.

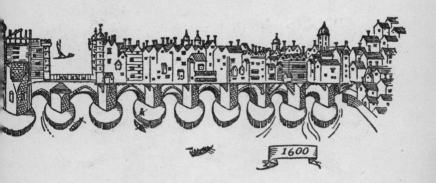

1600

Silver and gold will be stolen away,
   Dance over the Lady Lea;
Silver and gold will be stolen away,
   With a gay lady.

Then we must set a man to watch,
   Dance over the Lady Lea;
Then we must set a man to watch,
   With a gay lady.

Suppose the man should fall asleep?
   Dance over the Lady Lea;
Suppose the man should fall asleep?
   With a gay lady.

Then we must put a pipe in his mouth,
   Dance over the Lady Lea;
Then we must put a pipe in his mouth,
   With a gay lady.

TODAY

Suppose the pipe should fall and break?
 Dance over the Lady Lea;
Suppose the pipe should fall and break?
 With a gay lady.

Then we must set a dog to watch,
 Dance over the Lady Lea;
Then we must set a dog to watch,
 With a gay lady.

Suppose the dog should run away?
 Dance over the Lady Lea;
Suppose the dog should run away?
 With a gay lady.

Then we must chain him to a post,
 Dance over the Lady Lea;
Then we must chain him to a post,
 With a gay lady.

Hey diddle dinkety poppety pet,
The merchants of London they wear scarlet;
Silk in the collar and gold in the hem,
So merrily march the merchant men.

As I was going by Charing Cross,
I saw a black man upon a black horse;
They told me it was King Charles the First –
Oh dear, my heart was ready to burst!

Hey ding a ding, and ho ding a ding,
The parliament soldiers are gone to the king;
Some they did laugh, and some they did cry
To see the parliament soldiers go by.

Jog-Alongs

Father and Mother and Uncle John
Went to market one by one;
Father fell off —!
Mother fell off —!
But Uncle John went on, and on,
    and on, and on, and on.

The knee-king's mount collapses when father falls off, and when
mother falls off, but thereafter jogs on, and on, and on.

Mother and Father and Uncle Dick
Went to London on a stick;
The stick broke and made a smoke,
And stifled all the London folk.

To market, to market, to buy a plum bun,
Home again, home again, market is done.

To market, to market, a gallop, a trot,
To buy some good mutton to put in the pot.
Threepence a quarter, a shilling a side,
If it had not been killed, it would surely have died.

Trit trot to Boston, trit trot to Lynn,
Take care little boy – you don't fall in.

A farmer went trotting upon his grey mare,
    Bumpety, bumpety, bump!
With his daughter behind him so rosy and fair,
    Lumpety, lumpety, lump!

A raven cried, Croak! and they all tumbled down,
    Bumpety, bumpety, bump!
The mare broke her knees and the farmer his crown,
    Lumpety, lumpety, lump!

The mischievous raven flew laughing away,
    Bumpety, bumpety, bump!
And vowed he would serve them the same the next day,
    Lumpety, lumpety, lump!

The Misfortunes of Simple Simon

Simple Simon met a pieman
  Going to the fair;
Says Simple Simon to the pieman,
  Let me taste your ware.

Says the pieman to Simple Simon,
  Show me first your penny;
Says Simple Simon to the pieman,
  Indeed I have not any.

Simple Simon went a-fishing,
  For to catch a whale;
All the water he had got
  Was in his mother's pail.

Simple Simon went a-hunting,
  For to catch a hare;
He rode a goat about the streets,
  But couldn't find one there.

He went to catch a dickey bird,
    And thought he could not fail,
Because he'd got a little salt,
    To put upon its tail.

He went to shoot a wild duck,
    But wild duck flew away;
Says Simon, I can't hit him,
    Because he will not stay.

He went to ride a spotted cow,
    That had a little calf;
She threw him down upon the ground,
    Which made the people laugh.

Once Simon made a great snowball,
    And brought it in to roast;
He laid it down before the fire,
    And soon the ball was lost.

He went to try if cherries ripe
    Did grow upon a thistle;
He pricked his finger very much,
    Which made poor Simon whistle.

He went for water in a sieve,
    But soon it all ran through;
And now poor Simple Simon
    Bids you all adieu.

Ride a Cock-Horse

Ride a cock-horse to Banbury Cross,
To see a fine lady upon a white horse;
Rings on her fingers and bells on her toes,
And she shall have music wherever she goes.

Ride a cock-horse to Banbury Cross,
To buy little Johnny a galloping horse;
It trots behind, and it ambles before,
And Johnny shall ride till he can ride no more.

To market, to market, to buy a fat pig,
Home again, home again, jiggety jig;
To market, to market, to buy a fat hog,
Home again, home again, jiggety jog.

As I was going to Banbury
All on a summer day,
My wife had butter, eggs, and cheese,
And I had corn and hay.
Bob drove the kine, and Tom the swine,
Dick led the foal and mare;
I sold them all, then home again
We came from Banbury Fair.

Ride a cock-horse to Banbury Cross,
To see what Tommy can buy;
A penny white loaf, a penny white cake,
And a two-penny apple pie.

Too Many Cooks Spoil the Broth

There were three cooks of Colebrook,
And they fell out with our cook;
And all was for a pudding he took
From the three cooks of Colebrook.

Mary Ann, Mary Ann,
Make the porridge in a pan;
Make it thick, make it thin,
Make it any way you can.

Pat-a-cake, pat-a-cake, baker's man,
Bake me a cake as fast as you can;
Pat it and prick it, and mark it with B,
Put it in the oven for Baby and me.

Polly put the kettle on,
Polly put the kettle on,
Polly put the kettle on,
    We'll all have tea.

Sukey take it off again,
Sukey take it off again,
Sukey take it off again,
    They've all gone away.

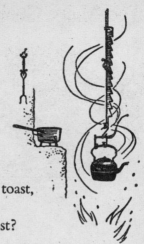

Blow the fire and make the toast,
Put the muffins on to roast,
Who is going to eat the most?
    We'll all have tea.

Oh dear, oh! My cake's all dough,
And how to make it better I do not know.

Pease porridge hot, pease porridge cold,
Pease porridge in the pot, nine days old.
Some like it hot, some like it cold,
Some like it in the pot, nine days old.

Hokey pokey winkey wum,
How do you like your 'taties done?
Fried in butter and stewed in rum,
Said the King of the Cannibal Islands.

Sing a Song of Sixpence

Sing a song of sixpence,
   A pocket full of rye;
Four and twenty blackbirds,
   Baked in a pie.

When the pie was opened,
   The birds began to sing;
Was not that a dainty dish,
   To set before the king?

The king was in his counting-house,
   Counting out his money;
The queen was in the parlour,
   Eating bread and honey.

The maid was in the garden,
   Hanging out the clothes,
Along came a blackbird,
   And snapped off her nose.

As it fell upon the ground
'Twas spied by Jenny Wren,
Who took a stick of sealing wax
And stuck it on again.

As they saw the nose stuck on
The maids cried out 'Hooray!'
Till someone said, 'But it is stuck
The topsy-turvy way!'

They took her to the King
Who just replied, 'What stuff!
'Tis better far put on that way,
So nice for taking snuff!'

They bought a pound of Lundyfoot
And threw it in her face.
She sneezed 'Achoo!' which twisted it
Into its proper place.

Believe It or Not

In a cottage in Fife
Lived a man and his wife,
Who, believe me, were comical folk;
For, to people's surprise,
They both saw with their eyes,
And their tongues moved whenever they spoke.

When quite fast asleep,
I've been told that to keep
Their eyes open they could not contrive;
They walked on their feet,
And 'twas thought what they eat
Helped, with drinking, to keep them alive.

Now what do you think
Of little Jack Jingle?
Before he was married
He used to live single.

The Wonderful Guinea-pig

There was a little guinea-pig,
Which, being little, was not big.
He always walked upon his feet,
And never fasted when he eat.

Though ne'er instructed by a cat,
He knew a mouse was not a rat;
He knew the good from naughty boys;
And when he squealed he made a noise.

When from a place he ran away,
He never at that place did stay;
And while he ran, as I am told,
He ne'er stood still for young or old.

One day I heard it gravely said,
That Master Guinea-pig was dead;
If that's the case, we safely may
Conclude he's not alive today.

Battles Royal

Oh, the mighty King of France,
  He marched his men to war;
But none of them got to the battlefield
  Because it was too far.

Oh, the brave old Duke of York,
  He had ten thousand men,
He marched them up to the top of the hill,
  And he marched them down again.
And when they were up they were up,
  And when they were down they were down,
And when they were only half way up,
  They were neither up nor down.

Here's Corporal Bull
A strong hearty fellow,
Who not used to fighting
Set up a loud bellow.

The Lion and the Unicorn
  Were fighting for the crown;
The Lion beat the Unicorn
  All about the town.
Some gave them white bread,
  And some gave them brown,
Some gave them plum cake,
  And sent them out of town.

Tweedledum and Tweedledee
  Agreed to have a battle,
For Tweedledum said Tweedledee
  Had spoiled his nice new rattle.
Just then flew by a monstrous crow,
  As big as a tar-barrel,
Which frightened both the heroes so,
  They quite forgot their quarrel.

Ten Little Injuns

Ten little Injuns
   Standing in a line,
One toddled home,
   And then there were nine.

Nine little Injuns
   Swinging on a gate,
One tumbled off,
   And then there were eight.

Eight little Injuns
   Never heard of heaven,
One went to sleep,
   And then there were seven.

Seven little Injuns
   Playing silly tricks,
One broke his neck,
   And then there were six.

Six little Injuns
   Kicking all alive,
One went to bed,
   And then there were five.

Five little Injuns
  On a cellar door,
One tumbled in,
  And then there were four.

Four little Injuns
  Out upon a spree,
One got sick,
  And then there were three.

Three little Injuns
  Out in a canoe,
One tumbled overboard,
  And then there were two.

Two little Injuns
  Fooling with a gun,
One shot the other,
  And then there was one.

One little Injun,
  With his little wife,
Lived in a wigwam
  The rest of his life.

One daddy Injun,
  One mammy squaw,
Soon raised a family
  Of ten Injuns more.

Sitting Down To It

Little Jack Horner
Sat in the corner,
Eating a Christmas pie;
He put in his thumb,
And pulled out a plum,
And said, What a good boy am I!

Little Polly Flinders
Sat among the cinders,
Warming her pretty little toes;
Her mother came and caught her,
And whipped her little daughter
For spoiling her nice new clothes.

Little Miss Muffet
Sat on a tuffet,
Eating her curds and whey;
There came a big spider,
Who sat down beside her
And frightened Miss Muffet away.

Little Miss Tuckett
Sat on a bucket,
Eating some peaches and cream;
There came a grasshopper
And tried hard to stop her;
But she said, Go away, or I'll scream.

71

Riddle-me-Rees

Riddle me, riddle me,
What is that:
Over the head
And under the hat?

I have long legs,
But short thighs,
A little head,
And no eyes.

Thirty white horses
Upon a white hill,
Now they dance,
Now they prance,
Now they stand still.

Patches and patches
Without any stitches;
If you tell me this riddle
I'll give you my breeches.

A little girl
Dressed in white,
Caught the fever
And died last night.

Tall and thin,
Red within,
Nail on top
And there it is.

I have a little sister
She lives near the ditch;
If you go near her
She gives you the itch.

A house full,
A hole full,
You cannot gather
A bowl full.

To find the answers fold the opposite page in half, and the left-hand column on page 74 will provide the answers to the right-hand column above; then turn the folded page over so that it half covers this one, and the answers to the left-hand column will be pictured beside each riddle.

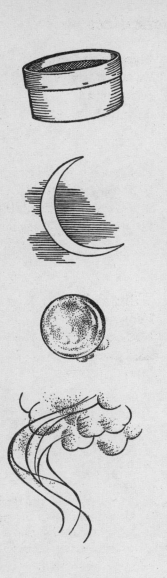

FOLD HERE

MIST

Riddle-me-Rees

Hoddy doddy,
With a round black body,
Three feet and a wooden
  hat.
Pray tell me what's that?

As round as a butter bowl,
As deep as a cup,
All the Mississippi river
Can't fill it up.

As round as a saucer,
As plump as a ball,
Can climb up the steeples,
And churches, and all.

As round as an apple,
As sharp as a lance,
If you go on its back
It will carry you to France.

As round as a biscuit,
As busy as a bee,
Prettiest little thing
You ever did see.

As light as a feather,
As round as a ball,
Yet all the king's men
Cannot carry it at all.

As round as a marble,
As flat as a pan,
The all of a woman,
The half of a man.

As high as a castle,
As weak as a wastle,
And all the king's horses
Cannot pull it down.

To find the answers fold the opposite page in half, and the right-hand column on page 73 will provide the answers to the left-hand column above; then turn the folded page over so that it half covers this one, and the answers to the right-hand column will be pictured beside each riddle.

Cock Robin

Who killed Cock Robin?
  I, said the Sparrow,
  With my bow and arrow,
I killed Cock Robin.

Who saw him die?
  I, said the Fly,
  With my little eye,
I saw him die.

Who caught his blood?
  I, said the Fish,
  With my little dish,
I caught his blood.

Who'll make his shroud?
  I, said the Beetle,
  With my thread and needle,
I'll make the shroud.

Who'll dig his grave?
  I, said the Owl,
  With my pick and shovel,
I'll dig his grave.

Who'll be the parson?
  I, said the Rook,
  With my little book,
I'll be the parson.

Who'll be the clerk?
  I, said the Lark,
  If it's not in the dark,
I'll be the clerk.

Who'll carry the link?
  I, said the Linnet,
  I'll fetch it in a minute,
I'll carry the link.

Who'll be chief mourner?
  I, said the Dove,
  I mourn for my love,
I'll be chief mourner

Who'll carry the coffin?
    I, said the Kite,
    If it's not through the night,
I'll carry the coffin.

Who'll bear the pall?
    We, said the Wren,
    Both the cock and the hen,
We'll bear the pall.

Who'll sing a psalm?
    I, said the Thrush,
    As she sat on a bush,
I'll sing a psalm.

Who'll toll the bell?
    I, said the Bull,
    Because I can pull,
So Cock Robin, farewell.

All the birds of the air
    Fell a-sighing and a-sobbing,
When they heard the bell toll
    For poor Cock Robin.

Two pigeons flying high,
Chinese vessel sailing by,
Weeping willow hanging o'er,
Bridge with three men, if not four,
Chinese mansion here it stands,
Seems to cover all the land,
An apple tree with apples on,
And a pretty fence to hang my song.

Ching-a-ring-a-ring-ching, Feast of Lanterns,
    What a lot of chopsticks, bombs and gongs;
Four-and-twenty thousand crinkum-crankums
    All among the bells and the ding dongs.

Golden Dreams

My mother sent me for some water,
For some water from the sea,
My foot slipped, and in I tumbled,
Three jolly sailors came to me:
One said he'd buy me silks and satins,
One said he'd buy me a guinea gold ring,
One said he'd buy me a silver cradle
For to rock my baby in.

If I had gold in goupins,
   If I had money in store,
If I had gold in goupins,
   My laddie should work no more.
He should have a maid to wait upon him,
   Another to curl his hair;
He should have a man to buckle his shoe,
   And then he should work no mair.

A bird in the air, a fish in the sea,
A bonnie wee lassie came singing to me;
The sun in the sky, the moon in a tree,
The bells in the steeple are ringing for me
     I went up the mountain
         And blew upon my horn,
       And every lad in Upper Town
         Knew that it was dawn.

I had a little nut tree,
   Nothing would it bear
But a silver nutmeg
   And a golden pear;
The king of Spain's daughter
   Came to visit me,
And all for the sake
   Of my little nut tree.

The Key of My Heart

Madam, I will give you a new lace cap,
With embroidery on the bottom and insertion at the top,
If you will be my bride, my joy, and only dear,
To walk and talk with me everywhere.

Sir, I will not accept of your new lace cap,
With embroidery on the bottom and insertion at the top,
I won't be your bride, your joy, and only dear,
To walk and talk with you everywhere.

Madam, I will give you a new silk gown,
With nineteen gold laces to lace it up and down,
If you will be my bride, my joy, and only dear,
To walk and talk with me everywhere.

Sir, I will not accept of your new silk gown,
With nineteen gold laces to lace it up and down,
I won't be your bride, your joy, and only dear,
To walk and talk with you everywhere.

Madam, I will give you a little silver bell,
To call up your servants if you should not feel well,
If you will be my bride, my joy, and only dear,
To walk and talk with me everywhere.

Sir, I will not accept of your little silver bell,
To call up my servants if I should not feel well,
I won't be your bride, your joy, and only dear,
To walk and talk with you everywhere.

Madam, I will give you a little greyhound,
Every hair upon its back worth a thousand pound,
If you will be my bride, my joy, and only dear,
To walk and talk with me everywhere.

Sir, I won't accept of your little greyhound,
With every hair upon its back worth a thousand pound,
I won't be your bride, your joy, and only dear,
To walk and talk with you everywhere.

Madam, I will give you the key of my heart,
To lock it up for ever, that we may never part,
If you will be my bride, my joy, and only dear,
To walk and talk with me everywhere.

Sir, I will accept of the key of your heart,
To lock it up for ever, that we may never part,
I will be your bride, your joy, and only dear,
To walk and talk with you everywhere.

Three Blind Mice

Three blind mice, see how they run!
They all ran after the farmer's wife,
Who cut off their tails with a carving knife,
Did you ever see such a thing in your life,
    As three blind mice?

Six little mice sat down to spin,
Pussy passed by, and she peeped in.
What are you doing, my little men?
We're weaving shirts for gentlemen.
Can I come in, and cut off your threads?
No, no, Mistress Pussy, you'll cut off our heads.

The little mouse doth skip and play

and Other Moosikies

Hickory, dickory, dock,
The mouse ran up the clock.
   The clock struck one,
   The mouse ran down,
Hickory, dickory, dock.

There was a wee bit moosikie
   That lived in pantry-attay O,
But it couldna get a bit o'cheese
   For cheekie-poussie-cattie O.
Said the moosie tae the cheesikie,
   O fain wad I be at ye O,
If it werena for the cruel paws
   O' cheekie-poussie-cattie O.

Pretty John Watts,
   We are troubled with rats,
Will you drive them out of the house?
   We have mice, too, in plenty,
   That feast in the pantry;
   But let them stay and nibble away;
What harm is a little brown mouse?

He runs by night and sleeps by day

The Old Woman in a Shoe

There was an old woman who lived in a shoe,
She had so many children she didn't know what to do;
She gave them some broth without any bread,
And whipped them all soundly and put them to bed.

Go to bed, Tom,
Go to bed, Tom,
Tired or not, Tom,
Go to bed, Tom.

and Other Old Women

There was an old woman,
　　And what do you think?
She lived upon nothing
　　But victuals and drink,
Victuals and drink
　　Were the chief of her diet,
And yet this old woman
　　Could never keep quiet.

There was an old woman lived under some stairs,
　　He, haw, haw, hum;
She sold apples and she sold pears,
　　He, haw, haw, hum.

All her bright money she laid on the shelf,
　　He, haw, haw, hum;
If you want any more, you may sing it yourself,
　　He, haw, haw, hum.

There was an old woman
　　Lived under a hill,
And if she's not gone
　　She lives there still.

Robin-a-Thrush

Robin he married a wife in the West,
  Moppety, moppety, mono,
And she turned out to be none of the best,
  With a high jig, jiggety, tops and petticoats,
  Robin-a-Thrush cries 'Mono!'

When she rises she gets up in haste,
  Moppety, moppety, mono,
And flies to the cupboard before she is laced,
  With a high jig, jiggety, tops and petticoats,
  Robin-a-Thrush cries 'Mono!'

She milks her cows but once a week,
  Moppety, moppety, mono,
And that's what makes her butter so sweet,
  With a high jig, jiggety, tops and petticoats,
  Robin-a-Thrush cries 'Mono!'

When she churns she churns in a boot,
    Moppety, moppety, mono,
And instead of a cruddle she puts in her foot,
    With a high jig, jiggety, tops and petticoats,
    Robin-a-Thrush cries 'Mono!'

She puts her cheese upon the shelf,
    Moppety, moppety, mono,
And leaves it to turn till it turns of itself,
    With a high jig, jiggety, tops and petticoats,
    Robin-a-Thrush cries 'Mono!'

It turned of itself and fell on the floor,
    Moppety, moppety, mono,
Got up on its feet and ran out of the door,
    With a high jig, jiggety, tops and petticoats,
    Robin-a-Thrush cries 'Mono!'

It ran till it came to Wakefield Cross,
    Moppety, moppety, mono,
And she followed after upon a white horse,
    With a high jig, jiggety, tops and petticoats,
    Robin-a-Thrush cries 'Mono!'

This song was made for gentlemen,
    Moppety, moppety, mono,
If you want any more, you must sing it again,
    With a high jig, jiggety, tops and petticoats,
    Robin-a-Thrush cries 'Mono!'

Woman's Work

Can you wash your father's shirt,
  Can you wash it clean?
Can you wash your father's shirt
  And bleach it on the green?
Yes, I can wash my father's shirt,
  And I can wash it clean.
I can wash my father's shirt
  And send it to the Queen.

They that wash on Monday
  Have all the week to dry;
They that wash on Tuesday
  Are not so much awry;
They that wash on Wednesday
  Are not so much to blame;
They that wash on Thursday
  Wash for very shame;
They that wash on Friday
  Wash in sorry need;
They that wash on Saturday
  Are lazy folk indeed.

The old woman must stand at the tub, tub, tub,
The dirty clothes to rub, rub, rub;
But when they are clean, and fit to be seen,
She'll dress like a lady and dance on the green.

I had a little wife,
 The prettiest ever seen;
She washed up the dishes
 And kept the house clean.

She went to the mill
 To fetch me some flour,
She brought it home safe
 In less than an hour.

She baked me my bread,
 She brewed me my ale,
She sat by the fire
 And told a fine tale.

Man's work lasts till set of sun,
Woman's work is never done.

Looking after Baby

Bye, baby bunting,
Father's gone a-hunting,
Mother's gone a-milking,
Sister's gone a-silking,
Brother's gone to buy a skin
To wrap the baby bunting in.

Diddle-me-diddle-me-dandy-O!
Diddle-me-diddle-me-darling.
If ever I do bake at the mill,
I'll bake little baby a parkin.

Warm, hands, warm,
The men are gone to plough,
If you want to warm your hands,
Warm your hands now.

Send Daddy home
With a fiddle and a drum,
A pocket full of sookies,
An apple and a plum.

Singing Baby to Sleep

Hush-a-bye, baby, on the tree top,
When the wind blows the cradle will rock;
When the bough breaks the cradle will fall,
Down will come baby, cradle, and all.

A YORKSHIRE LULLABY

Rock-a-boo babby, babbies is bonny,
Two in a cradle, three is too monny,
Four is a company, five is a charge,
Six is a family, seven's too large.

A SCOTTISH LULLABY

Lay doon yer little heidie
In yer cosy cradle beddie,
Shut yer eenies an close yer mouie,
An' sleep for siller tae buy a cooie,
My bonnie baby.

Bo-peep's Sheep

Little Bo-peep
Has lost her sheep,
And doesn't know where to find them;
Leave them alone,
And they'll come home,
Bringing their tails behind them.

Little Bo-peep
Fell fast asleep,
And dreamt she heard them bleating;
But when she awoke,
She found it a joke,
For they were still a-fleeting.

Then up she took
Her little crook,
Determined for to find them;
She found them indeed,
But it made her heart bleed,
For they'd left their tails behind them.

Mary's Lamb

Mary had a little lamb,
   Its fleece was white as snow;
And everywhere that Mary went
   The lamb was sure to go.

It followed her to school one day,
   That was against the rule;
It made the children laugh and play
   To see a lamb at school.

And so the teacher turned it out,
   But still it lingered near;
And waited patiently about
   Till Mary did appear.

Why does the lamb love Mary so?
   The eager children cry;
Why, Mary loves the lamb, you know,
   The teacher did reply.

Country Symphony

Rats in the garden, catch 'em Towser,
Cows in the cornfield, run, boys, run;
Cat's in the cream pot, stop her, now sir,
Fire on the mountain, run, boys, run.

The cock's on the house-top,
   Blowing his horn;
The bull's in the barn,
   A-threshing the corn;
The maids in the meadow
   Are making the hay;
The ducks in the river
   Are swimming away.

I went up the high hill,
There I saw a climbing goat;
I went down by the running rill,
There I saw a ragged sheep;
I went out to the roaring sea,
There I saw a tossing boat;
I went under the green tree,
There I saw two doves asleep.

The hart he loves the high wood,
The hare she loves the hill;
The knight he loves his bright sword,
The lady loves her will.

Cheese and bread for gentlemen,
Corn and hay for horses,
Tobacco for the auld wives,
And kisses for the lasses.

97

SONG OF THE MILLER

There was a jolly miller once,
   Lived by the river Dee;
He worked and sang from morn till night,
   No lark more blithe than he.
And this the burden of his song
   Forever used to be,
I care for nobody, no! not I,
   If nobody cares for me.

SONG OF THE OLD MAN

When I was young and in my prime,
I'd done my work by dinner time;
But now I'm old and cannot trot
I'm obliged to work till eight o'clock.

Earning a Living

Little Tommy Tucker
   Sings for his supper:
What shall we give him?
   White bread and butter.
How shall he cut it
   Without a knife?
How will he be married
   Without a wife?

    See-saw, Margery Daw,
    Jacky shall have a new master;
    Jacky shall have but a penny a day,
    Because he can't work any faster.

    When Jacky's a good boy,
    He shall have cakes and custard;
    But when he does nothing but cry,
    He shall have nothing but mustard.

God made man, and man makes money,
God made the bees, and the bees make honey.
God made a little man to plough and to sow,
God made a little boy to keep away the crow.
God made a woman to brew and to bake,
God made a little maid to eat plum cake.

The Old Man from
over the Lea

There was an old man came over the lea,
    Ha, ha, ha, ha! but I won't have him!
He came with a purse of gold wooing to me,
    With his hard beard newly shaven.

My mother she bid me open the door;
    Ha, ha, ha, ha! but I won't have him!
I opened the door, and he fell on the floor,
    With his hard beard newly shaven.

My mother she bid me give him some pie;
    Ha, ha, ha, ha! but I won't have him!
I gave him some pie, and he laid the crust by,
    With his hard beard newly shaven.

My mother she bid me give him a stool;
    Ha, ha, ha, ha! but I won't have him!
I gave him a stool, and he looked like a fool,
    With his hard beard newly shaven.

My mother she bid me take him to church;
    Ha, ha, ha, ha! but I won't have him!
I took him to church but left him in the lurch,
    With his hard beard newly shaven.

The Jacket and
the Petticoat

As I went by my little pig-sty,
I saw a child's petticoat hanging to dry,
    Hanging to dry, hanging to dry,
I saw a child's petticoat hanging to dry.

I took off my jacket and hung it close by,
To bear that petticoat company,
    Company, company,
To bear that petticoat company.

The wind blew high and down they fell,
Jacket and petticoat into the well,
    Into the well, into the well,
Jacket and petticoat into the well.

Oh! says the jacket, we shall be drowned;
No, says the petticoat, we shall be found,
    We shall be found, we shall be found,
No, says the petticoat, we shall be found.

A miller passed by, and they gave a loud shout,
He put in his hand and he pulled them both out,
    Pulled them both out, pulled them both out,
He put in his hand and he pulled them both out.

Alarms and Accidents

Ding, dong, bell, pussy's in the well.
Who put her in? Little Johnny Green.
Who pulled her out? Little Tommy Stout.
What a naughty boy was that,
To try to drown poor pussy cat,
Who never did any harm,
But killed the mice in his father's barn.

Bryan O'Lynn and his wife and wife's mother,
They all went over a bridge together;
The bridge broke down, and they all tumbled in,
We'll go home by water, said Bryan O'Lynn.

Jack and Jill went up the hill,
  To fetch a pail of water;
Jack fell down, and broke his crown,
  And Jill came tumbling after.

Goosey, goosey gander,
  Whither shall I wander?
Upstairs and downstairs
  And in my lady's chamber.
There I met an old man
  Who would not say his prayers,
I took him by the left leg
  And threw him down the stairs.

Humpty Dumpty

Humpty Dumpty sat on a wall,
Humpty Dumpty had a great fall;
   All the king's horses,
   And all the king's men,
Couldn't put Humpty together again.

Usual version

Humpty Dumpty sat on a wall,
Humpty Dumpty had a great fall;
Four score men, and four score more,
Cannot put Humpty Dumpty where he
   was before.

Old version

Humpty Dumpty ligs in t' beck
Wid a white counterpane aroon his neck;
Forty doctors and forty wrights
Will nivver put Humpty Dumpty to rights.

Cumberland version
ligs in t' beck: lies in the brook

Humpty Dumpty and his brother
Were as like as one another,
Couldn't tell one from t'other
Humpty Dumpty and his brother.

Somerset version

Humpty Dumpty went to town,
Humpty Dumpty tore his gown;
All the needles in the town
Couldn't mend Humpty Dumpty's gown.

American version

Humpty Dumpty sat on a spoon,
Humpty will go in the egg cup soon;
And all the paste and all the glue
Will not make Humpty look like new.

Schoolchild version

Wirgele-Wargele, auf der Bank,
Fällt es 'runter, ist es krank,
Ist kein Doktor im ganzen Land,
Der dem Wirgele-Wargele helfen kann.

German version

I saw a peacock with a fiery tail
I saw a blazing comet drop down hail
I saw a cloud with ivy circled round
I saw a sturdy oak creep on the ground
I saw a pismire swallow up a whale
I saw a raging sea brim full of ale
I saw a Venice glass sixteen foot deep
I saw a well full of men's tears that weep
I saw their eyes all in a flame of fire
I saw a house as big as the moon and higher
I saw the sun even in the midst of night
I saw the man that saw this wondrous sight.

a pismire: an ant.

I saw a fishpond all on fire
I saw a house bow to a squire
I saw a parson twelve feet high
I saw a cottage near the sky
I saw a balloon made of lead
I saw a coffin drop down dead
I saw a sparrow run a race
I saw two horses making lace
I saw a girl just like a cat
I saw a kitten wear a hat
I saw a man who saw these too,
And says, though strange, they all are true.

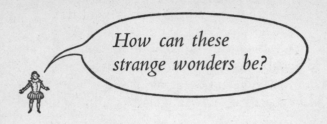

How can these
strange wonders be?

I saw a pack of cards gnawing a bone
I saw a dog seated on Britain's throne
I saw the Queen shut up within a box
I saw a shilling driving a fat ox
I saw a man lying in a muff all night
I saw a glove reading news by candle-light
I saw a woman not a twelvemonth old
I saw a greatcoat all of solid gold
I saw two buttons telling of their dreams
I heard my friends, who wish'd I'd quit these themes.

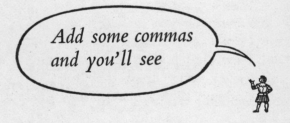

Add some commas
and you'll see

Mysteries Unravelled

There was a man who went to the fair,
He bought three horses and one was a mare;
One was blind and one couldn't see,
And t'other had its head where its tail should be.

[The third horse was tied to the manger by its tail.]

There was a king met a king
    In a narrow lane;
Said the king to the king,
    Where have you been?
I have been a-hunting
    The buck and the doe.
Will you lend me your dog?
    Yes, I will do so;
Call upon him, call upon him.
    What is his name?
I have told you once
    And won't tell you again.

[The dog's name was Bean, Ben, or Bin, according
to pronunciation.]

Long man legless, came to the door staffless,
Crying, Guidwife! keep in your cocks and hens;
For cats and dogs I care na.

[A worm has reason to fear chickens but not cats and dogs.]

Two legs sat upon three legs
With one leg in his lap;
In comes four legs
And runs away with one leg;
Up jumps two legs,
Catches up three legs,
Throws it after four legs,
And makes him bring back one leg.

[A man sat on a three-legged stool with a leg of mutton on his lap. In comes a dog and runs away with the mutton. Up jumps the man, throws the stool at the dog, and makes him bring back the mutton.]

Without a bridle or a saddle,
Across a thing I ride a-straddle;
And those I ride, by help of me,
Though almost blind are made to see.

[A pair of spectacles.]

I've seen you where you never were,
And where you ne'er will be,
And yet within that self-same place
You can be seen by me.

[In a looking-glass.]

Tell me, ladies, if you can,
Who is this highly favoured man?
Although he marries many a wife
He still keeps single all his life.

[A parson.]

Pop Goes the Weasel!

Up and down the City Road,
In and out the Eagle,
That's the way the money goes,
Pop goes the weasel!

A ha'penny for a cotton ball,
A farthing for a needle,
That's the way the money goes,
Pop goes the weasel!

Half a pound of tuppenny rice,
Half a pound of treacle,
Mix it up and make it nice,
Pop goes the weasel!

Every time my mother goes out,
The monkey's on the table,
Cracking nuts and eating spice,
Pop goes the weasel!

If you want to buy a pig,
Buy a pig with hairs on,
Every hair a penny a pair,
Pop goes the weasel!

Overheads

Gregory Griggs, Gregory Griggs,
Had twenty-seven different wigs.
He wore them up, he wore them down,
To please the people of the town;
He wore them east, he wore them west,
But he never could tell which he loved the best.

Yankee Doodle came to town,
 Riding on a pony;
He stuck a feather in his cap
 And called it macaroni.

Barber, barber, shave a pig,
How many hairs to make a wig?
Four-and-twenty, that's enough.
Give the barber a pinch of snuff.

Hickety, pickety, i-silikety, pompalorum jig,
Every man who has no hair generally wears a wig.

A Drove of Donkeys

Donkey, donkey, old and grey,
Open your mouth and gently bray,
Lift your ears and blow your horn,
To wake the world this sleepy morn.

Donkey, donkey, do not bray,
But mend your pace and trot away;
Indeed, the market's almost done,
My butter's melting in the sun.

Gee up, Neddy, to the fair,
What shall I buy when I get there?
A ha'penny apple, a penny pear.
Gee-up, Neddy, to the fair.

A RIDDLE

This being's most despised by man,
Yet does him all the good he can;
And bore the greatest Prince on earth,
Who gave to righteousness new birth.

If I had a donkey
    And he wouldn't go,
D'you think I'd wallop him?
    Oh, no, no.
I'd put him in the barn
    And give him some corn,
The best little donkey
    That ever was born.

Up in the North, a long way off,
The donkey's got the whooping cough;
He whooped so hard with the whooping cough,
He whooped his head and his tail right off.

Come out to Play

Girls and boys come out to play,
The moon is shining bright as day;
Leave your supper, and leave your sleep,
And come with your playfellows into the street;
Come with a whoop, and come with a call,
Come with a good will, or come not at all,
Come let us dance on the open green,
And she who holds longest shall be our queen.

Ring-a-ring o' roses,
A pocket full of posies.
A-tishoo! A-tishoo!
We all fall down.

Ring-a-ring o' roses,
A pocket full of posies,
One for you, and one for me,
And one for little Moses.
A-tishoo! A-tishoo! We'll all fall down.

Ring-a-ring o' roses,
A pocket full of posies,
Hush-a, hush-a, we all fall down.
Cows are in the meadow,
Lying fast asleep,
Hush-a, hush-a, we all jump up.

The moon shines bright,
The stars give a light,
You may play at any game
At ten o'clock at night.

Here we go round by jinga-ring,
    Jinga-ring, jinga-ring,
Here we go round by jinga-ring,
    About the merry ma tanzie.

A lump of gold to tell her name,
    Tell her name, tell her name,
A lump of gold to tell her name,
    About the merry ma tanzie.

A bottle of wine to tell his name,
    Tell his name, tell his name,
A bottle of wine to tell his name,
    About the merry ma tanzie.

Sweep the house till the bride comes home,
    The bride comes home, the bride comes home,
Sweep the house till the bride comes home,
    About the merry ma tanzie.

So Long at the Fair

Oh dear, what can the matter be?
Dear, dear, what can the matter be?
Oh dear, what can the matter be?
Johnny's so long at the fair.

He promised he'd buy me a fairing should please me,
And then for a kiss, oh! he vowed he would tease me,
He promised he'd bring me a bunch of blue ribbons
To tie up my bonny brown hair.

And it's Oh dear, what can the matter be?
Dear, dear, what can the matter be?
Oh dear, what can the matter be?
Johnny's so long at the fair.

He promised to buy me a pair of sleeve buttons,
A pair of new garters that cost him but tuppence,
He promised he'd bring me a bunch of blue ribbons
To tie up my bonny brown hair.

THE RECRUITING SERGEANT

Come here to me, my merry, merry men,
  Said a sergeant at the fair;
And the bumpkins all were very merry men,
  And they all came running there.
Fat and spare, round and square,
  See them stare with noddles bare,
And the piper piped an air,
  And the drummer drummed his share,
With a rub-a-dub, rub-a-dub, row dow dow,
And the little dogs answered bow, wow, wow,
  And the boys cried out Hurrah!
  Hurrah! Hurrah! Hurrah!

Close Relations

Noah of old three babies had,
Or grown-up children, rather;
Shem, Ham, and Japeth, they were called,
Now who was Japeth's father?

Brothers and sisters have I none,
But that man's father is my father's son.

If Dick's father is John's son,
What relation is Dick to John?

There were three sisters in a hall
Then came a knight amongst them all;
Good morrow, aunt, to the one,
Good morrow, aunt, to the other,
Good morrow, gentlewoman, to the third,
If you were an aunt, as the other two be,
I would say good morrow, then, aunts all three.

The first puzzle is as simple as asking 'Who was the father of Zebedee's son?' The rhyme itself says that Japeth's father was Noah. The other three puzzles may require more working out, but we hope it will be agreed that the man who points at the son of his father's son is pointing at his own son; that Dick is John's grandson; and that the third sister is not an aunt because she is the knight's mother.

Fair Shares

The fiddler and his wife,
   The piper and his mother,
Ate three half-cakes, three whole cakes,
   And three quarters of another.

The parson, his wife,
   The clerk and his sister,
Went down to the meadow
   All of a clister.
They found a bird's nest
   With four eggs in it,
They took one each
   And left one in it.

Elizabeth, Elspeth, Betsy, and Bess,
   They all went together to seek a bird's nest;
They found a bird's nest with five eggs in,
   They all took one and left four in.

If the fiddler's wife and the piper's mother are one and the same person the division of the cakes was not difficult. Likewise if the clerk's sister has the happiness to be married to the parson there were only three bird's-nesters. Thirdly, since Elspeth, Betsy, and Bess are pet-names for Elizabeth, it is probable that Lizzie (alias Eliza, Elsie, Tetty, Betty, or Beth) was bird's-nesting on her own.

Old King Cole's Band

Old King Cole was a merry old soul,
And a merry old soul was he;
He called for his pipe,
And he called for his bowl,
And he called for his fiddlers three.

Each fiddler he had a fiddle,
And the fiddles went tweedle-dee;
Oh, there's none so rare as can compare
With King Cole and his fiddlers three.

Then he called for his fifers two,
And they puffed and they blew tootle-oo;
And King Cole laughed as his glass he quaffed,
And his fifers puffed tootle-oo.

Then he called for his drummer boy,
The army's pride and joy,
And the thuds out-rang with a loud bang! bang!
The noise of the noisiest toy.

Then he called for his trumpeters four,
Who stood at his own palace door,
And they played trang-a-tang
Whilst the drummer went bang,
And King Cole he called for more.

He called for a man to conduct,
Who into his bed had been tuck'd,
And he had to get up without bite or sup
And waggle his stick and conduct.

Old King Cole laughed with glee,
Such rare antics to see;
There never was a man in merry England
Who was half as merry as he.

Slug-a-Beds

Elsie Marley is grown so fine,
She won't get up to feed the swine,
But lies in bed till eight or nine.
  Lazy Elsie Marley.

Robin and Richard
  Were two pretty men,
They lay in bed
  Till the clock struck ten;
Then up starts Robin
  And looks at the sky,
Oh, brother Richard,
  The sun's very high.
The steamer has gone,
  We can't get a ride,
You carry the wallet,
  I'll run by your side.

To bed, to bed,
Says Sleepy-head;
Let's bide a while, says Slow;
Put on the pot,
Says Greedy-gut,
We'll sup before we go.

Rock, rock, bubbly jock,
Wake me up at ten o'clock;
Ten o'clock is far too soon,
Wake me up in the afternoon.

A diller, a dollar,
A ten o'clock scholar,
What makes you come so soon?
You used to come at ten o'clock,
But now you come at noon.

Lazy Zany Addlepate,
Go to bed early and get up late.

Sluggardy-guise, sluggardy-guise,
Loth to go to bed and loth to rise.

These Little Pigs

This little pig went to market,
This little pig stayed at home,
This little pig had roast beef,
And this little pig had none,
And this little pig went wee–wee–wee
    all the way home.

Whose little pigs are these, these, these,
    And whose little pigs are these?
They are Johnny Cook's, I know by their looks,
    I found them among the peas.
Go pound them, go pound them.
    I dare not for my life;
For, though I don't love Johnny Cook,
    I dearly love his wife.

This little pig said, I want some corn.
This little pig said, Where are you going to get it?
This little pig said, Out of Master's barn.
This little pig said, I'll go and tell.
And this little pig said, Queeky, queeky,
    I can't get over the barn door sill.

There was a lady loved a swine,
   Honey, quoth she,
Pig-hog, wilt thou be mine?
   Hoogh, quoth he.

I'll build thee a silver sty,
   Honey, quoth she,
And in it thou shalt lie.
   Hoogh, quoth he.

Pinned with a silver pin,
   Honey, quoth she,
That you may go out and in.
   Hoogh, quoth he.

Wilt thou have me now,
   Honey? quoth she.
Speak or my heart will break.
   Hoogh, quoth he.

The Queen of Hearts and
the Stolen Tarts

The Queen of Hearts she made some tarts,
    All on a summer's day;
The Knave of Hearts he stole those tarts,
    And took them quite away.

The Queen of Hearts had made those tarts
    To feast a chosen few;
And on the shelf put them herself,
    Saying 'They'll surely do.'
For she'd sent out her cards about
    To every King and Queen,
Who in the pack, in red and black,
    Are always to be seen.

Each noble pair in state came there,
    The royal board was spread;
The King with verve began to serve,
    The Queen she cut the bread.
The soup and fish, and many a dish,
    They ate with laughter gay,
And now the plum-pudding was come,
    As though 'twere Christmas day.

The Queen calls for the tarts

The Queen called then her serving men,
    Unconscious of disaster;
'Remove,' said she, 'this dish from me,
    And put it to your master.'
All wondered what else she had got,
    When to their joy she bade
The Knave of Hearts to bring the tarts
    Which she herself had made.

The Knave he went as he'd been sent,
    But soon returned to say,
'Some malcontent on thieving bent
    Has stole the tarts away.'
Oh then each guest did try his best
    A cheerful look to wear,
As if to say, 'Don't mind it, pray,
    We really do not care.'

The Knave blames the cat

Then spoke the Knave in accents grave,
  'Your Majesty,' said he,
'I think I know who is the foe –
  Your tom cat it must be;
He looked at me quite guiltily,
  And ran away full speed,
Which surely shows he full well knows
  'Twas he who did the deed.'

Then from his seat in anger great,
  Up rose the King of Hearts:
'Oh, Knave, for shame!' he did exclaim,
  'Do cats eat damson tarts?
It's my belief thou art the thief,
  But that I soon will see;
So go and call my servants all,
  And bid them come to me.'

The maids and serving men assemble

Up bustled then the serving men,
    Up bustled all the maids;
And there they stand a goodly band,
    According to their grades.
The Knave, 'tis said, was at their head,
    For he was reckoned chief:
'Now by this ring,' exclaimed the King,
    'I'll soon find out the thief.'

The maidens then, and serving men,
    Stared at the King of Hearts:
'I see,' said he, right solemnly,
    'Who stole the damson tarts:
His lips retain the purple stain
    Of juice upon them yet;
To hide his sin, his mouth and chin
    To wipe, he did forget.'

The Knave's guilt is established

All looked to see who it could be,
　　Except the Knave, I wot,
Who did begin to wipe his chin,
　　Though it no stain had got.
Oh then up starts the King of Hearts,
　　'Deceitful Knave!' cried he,
'Now straight confess your wickedness,
　　Upon your bended knee.'

Up rose the Queen with bitter mien,
　　'Oh Sire!' she cried, 'did I
Prepare a treat for Knaves to eat?
　　He surely ought to die.'
The King looked grave at Queen and Knave,
　　Quoth he, 'The tarts are eaten;
But mercy still shall be my will,
　　So let the thief be beaten.'

Nick-Nock, Padlock

There was an old woman and she went one,
She went nick-nock up against a gun.

Nick-nock, padlock, sing a little song,
See the little ploughboys troddling along.

There was an old woman and she went two,
She went nick-nock up against a shoe.

There was an old woman and she went three,
She went nick-nock up against a tree.

There was an old woman and she went four,
She went nick-nock up against a door.

There was an old woman and she went five,
She went nick-nock up against a hive.

There was an old woman and she went six,
She went nick-nock up against some sticks.

There was an old woman and she went seven,
She went nick-nock up against eleven.

There was an old woman and she went eight,
She went nick-nock up against a gate.

There was an old woman and she went nine,
She went nick-nock up against a line.

There was an old woman and she went ten,
She went nick-nock up against a hen.

Gluttons and

Hannah Bantry, in the pantry,
Gnawing at a mutton bone;
How she gnawed it, how she clawed it,
When she found herself alone.

Charlie Wag, Charlie Wag,
Ate the pudding and swallowed the bag.

John Bull, John Bull,
Your belly's so full,
You can't jump over
A three-legged stool.

Deedle deedle dumpling, my son John,
Ate a pasty five feet long;
He bit it once, he bit it twice,
Oh, my goodness, it was full of mice!

'Platter Champions'

Jack Sprat could eat no fat,
　　His wife could eat no lean,
And so between them both, you see,
　　They licked the platter clean.

Round about, round about, applety pie,
My daddy loves good ale, and so do I.
Up, mammy, up, and fill us a cup,
And daddy and I will sup it all up.

Robin and Bobbin, two big-bellied men,
They ate more victuals than three-score and ten;
They ate a cow, they ate a calf,
They ate a butcher and a half,
They ate a church, they ate a steeple,
They ate the priest and all the people,
And still complained they were not full.

Consequences

I went down the garden
And there I found a farden;
I gave it to my mother
To buy a little brother;
My brother was so cross
They put him on a horse;
The horse was so dandy
They gave him a drop of brandy;
The brandy was so strong
They put him in a pond;
The pond was so deep
They put him on a heap;
The heap was so high
They put him in a pie;
The pie was so hot
They put him in a pot;
The pot was so little
They put him in a kettle;
The kettle had a spout
And they all jumped out.

Anna Maria she sat on the fire;
The fire was too hot, she sat on the pot;
The pot was too round, she sat on the ground;
The ground was too flat, she sat on the cat;
The cat ran away with Maria on her back.

When I was a lad as big as my Dad,
I jumped into a pea-swad;
Pea-swad was so full,
I jumped into a roaring bull;
Roaring bull was so fat,
I jumped into a gentleman's hat;
Gentleman's hat was so fine,
I jumped into a bottle of wine;
Bottle of wine was so clear,
I jumped into a bottle of beer;
Bottle of beer was so thick,
I jumped into a knobbed stick;
Knobbed stick wouldn't bend,
I jumped into a turkey hen;
Turkey hen wouldn't lay,
I jumped into a piece of clay;
Piece of clay was so nasty,
I jumped into an apple pasty;
Apple pasty was so good,
I jumped into a lump of wood;
Lump of wood was so rotten,
I jumped into a bale of cotton;
The bale of cotton set on fire,
Blew me up to Jeremiah;
Jeremiah was a prophet,
Had a horse and couldn't stop it;
Horse knocked against t'ould cobbler's door,
Knocked t'ould cobbler on the floor;
Cobbler with his rusty gun
Shot the horse and off it run.

Astronauts

What's the news of the day,
Good neighbour, I pray?
They say a balloon
Is gone up to the moon.

On Saturday night I lost my wife,
And where do you think I found her?
Up in the moon, singing a tune,
And all the stars around her.

Dickery, dickery, dare,
The pig flew up in the air;
The man in brown soon brought him down,
Dickery, dickery, dare.

Sing, sing, what shall I sing?
Mary Ann Cotton tied up on a string.
Where? Where? Up in the air;
Selling black puddings a penny a pair.

ENGLISH

There was an old woman tossed up in a basket,
  Seventeen times as high as the moon;
And where she was going, I couldn't but ask it,
  For in her hand she carried a broom.
Old woman, old woman, old woman, quoth I,
  O whither, O whither, O whither so high?
To sweep the cobwebs off the sky!
  Shall I go with you? Aye, by-and-by.

SCOTTISH

There was a wee wifie row't up in a blanket,
  Nineteen times as hie as the moon;
And what did she there I canna declare,
  For in her oxter she bure the sun.
Wee wifie, wee wifie, wee wifie, quo' I,
  O what are ye doin' up there sae hie?
I'm blawin' the cauld cluds out o' the sky.
  Weel dune, weel dune, wee wifie! quo' I.

137

The Frog and the Crow

There was a jolly frog in the river did swim, O!
And a comely black crow lived by the river brim, O!
    Come on shore, come on shore,
      Said the crow to the frog, and then, O!
    No, you'll bite me, no, you'll bite me,
      Said the frog to the crow again, O!

But there is sweet music on yonder green hill, O!
And you'll be a dancer, a dancer in yellow,
    All in yellow, all in yellow,
      Said the crow to the frog, and then, O!
    All in yellow, all in yellow,
      Said the frog to the crow again, O!

Farewell, ye little fishes, farewell every good fellow,
For I'm going to be a dancer, a dancer in yellow.
    Oh beware, take care,
      Said the fish to the frog, and then, O!
    All in yellow, all in yellow,
      Said the frog to the fish again, O!

The frog he came swimming, a-swimming to land, O!
The crow he came hopping to lend him a hand, O!
    Sir, I thank you, sir, I thank you,
      Said the frog to the crow, and then, O!
    You are welcome, most welcome,
      Said the crow to the frog again, O!

But where is the music on yonder green hill, O?
And where are the dancers, the dancers in yellow?
    All in yellow, all in yellow,
      Said the frog to the crow again, O!
    They are here, said the crow,
      And ate him up there and then, O!

Pussies at the Fireside

The cat sat asleep by the side of the fire,
   The mistress snored loud as a pig;
Jack took up his fiddle by Jenny's desire,
   And struck up a bit of a jig.

Pussy at the fireside suppin' up brose,
Down came a cinder and burned pussy's nose.
Oh, said pussy, that's no fair.
Well, said the cinder, you shouldn't be there.

Pussy cat sits beside the fire,
   So pretty and so fair.
In walks the little dog,
   Ah, Pussy, are you there?
How do you do, Mistress Pussy?
   Mistress Pussy, how do you do?
I thank you kindly, little dog,
   I'm very well just now.

Pussies in the Pantry

Hie, hie, says Anthony,
Puss is in the pantry,
Gnawing, gnawing, a mutton mutton-bone;
See how she tumbles it,
See how she mumbles it,
See how she tosses the mutton mutton-bone.

Pussy cat ate the dumplings,
Pussy cat ate the dumplings;
Mamma stood by, and cried, Oh, fie!
Why did you eat the dumplings?

Rindle, randle,
Light the candle,
The cat's among the pies;
No matter for that,
The cat'll get fat,
And I'm too lazy to rise.

The Story of the Little Market Woman

There was a little woman,
　As I have heard tell,
She went to market
　Her eggs for to sell,
She went to market
　All on a market day,
And she fell asleep
　On the King's highway.

There came by a pedlar
　His name was Stout,
He cut her petticoats
　All round about;
He cut her petticoats
　Up to her knees,
Which made the poor woman
　To shiver and sneeze.

When the little woman
　Began to awake,
She began to shiver,
　And she began to shake;
She began to shake,
　And she began to cry,
Goodness mercy on me,
　This is none of I!

If it be not I,
  As I suppose it be,
I have a little dog at home,
  And he knows me;
If it be I,
  He'll wag his little tail,
And if it be not I,
  He'll loudly bark and wail.

Home went the little woman,
  All in the dark,
Up jumped the little dog,
  And he began to bark,
He began to bark,
  And she began to cry,
Goodness mercy on me,
  I see I be not I!

This poor little woman
  Passed the night on a stile,
She shivered with cold,
  And she trembled the while;
She slept not a wink
  But was all night awake,
And was heartily glad
  When the morning did break.

There came by the pedlar
  Returning from town,
She asked him for something
  To match her short gown,
The sly pedlar rogue
  Showed the piece he'd purloined,
Said he to the woman,
  It will do nicely joined.

She pinned on the piece,
  And exclaimed, What a match!
I am lucky indeed
  Such a bargain to catch.
The dog wagged his tail,
  And she began to cry,
Goodness mercy on me,
  I've discovered it be I!

Rogues and Vagabonds

Hark, hark, the dogs do bark,
  The beggars are coming to town;
Some in rags, and some in jags,
  And one in a velvet gown.

Taffy is a Welshman,
Taffy is a thief,
Taffy came to my house
And stole a golden leaf.
I went to Taffy's house
Taffy wasn't in,
I went into Taffy's house
And stole a golden pin.

I had a little moppety, I put it in my pockety,
  And fed it on corn and hay;
By came a beggar and swore he would have her,
  And stole my little moppety away.

Bow, Wow, Wow

Bow, wow, wow,
Whose dog art thou?
I'm Mother Hubbard's dog,
Bow, wow, wow.

Old Mother Hubbard, she went to the cupboard
  To fetch her poor dog a bone,
But when she got there, the cupboard was bare,
  And so the poor dog had none.

Two little dogs sat by the fire,
  In a basket of coal-dust;
Says one little dog to the other little dog,
  If you don't speak then I must.

I had a dog and his name was Dandy,
His tail was long and his legs were bandy,
His eyes were brown and his coat was sandy,
The best in the world was my dog Dandy.

I had a little dog,
    And his name was Bluebell,
I gave him some work,
    And he did it very well;
I sent him upstairs
    To pick up a pin,
He stepped in the coal-scuttle
    Up to his chin;
I sent him to the garden
    To pick some sage,
He tumbled down
    And fell in a rage;
I sent him to the cellar,
    To draw a pot of beer,
He came up again
    And said there was none there.

The Long Way to Wealth

My grandfather died
   and he left me a cow,
He told me to milk it
   but I didn't know how.
Wim-wam, wim-wam, Johnny put the saddle on,
I'm the boy for loping on.

I sold my cow
   and bought a calf,
It used to play
   at 'Footit and Half'.
Wim-wam, wim-wam, Johnny put the saddle on,
I'm the boy for loping on.

I sold my calf
   and bought a pig,
Which used to lope
   over Sowerby Brigg.
Wim-wam, wim-wam, Johnny put the saddle on,
I'm the boy for loping on.

I sold my pig
   and bought a hen,
It used to lay,
   but I didn't know when.
Wim-wam, wim-wam, Johnny put the saddle on,
I'm the boy for loping on.

or, The Loping Yorkshire Lad

I sold my hen
   and bought a dog,
Which used to play
   with my grandfather's clog.
Wim-wam, wim-wam, Johnny put the saddle on,
I'm the boy for loping on.

     I sold my dog
       and bought a cat,
     Which used to play
       with my grandfather's hat.
Wim-wam, wim-wam, Johnny put the saddle on,
I'm the boy for loping on.

I sold my cat
   and bought a mouse,
Which used to play
   all over the house.
Wim-wam, wim-wam, Johnny put the saddle on,
I'm the boy for loping on.

     If you want any more
       you must sing it yoursen,
     I might sing it again,
       but I don't know when.
Wim-wam, wim-wam, Johnny put the saddle on,
I'm the boy for loping on.

'Ifs' and 'Ans'

If 'ifs' and 'ans' were pots and pans
There'd be no work for tinkers.
If herrings grew on a blackberry bush
Then we should all be drinkers.

If all the world were paper,
And all the sea were ink,
If all the trees were bread and cheese,
What should we have to drink?

If all the seas were one sea,
What a great sea it would be;
And if all the trees were one tree,
What a great tree it would be;
And if this tree were to fall into the sea,
My! What a splish-splash there would be.

If wishes were horses
Beggars would ride.
If slatestones were buttercakes
They'd bite off the side.

A man in the wilderness asked me,
How many strawberries grew in the sea.
I answered him, as I thought good,
As many red herrings as swim in the wood.

Mother, may I go out to swim?
Yes, my darling daughter,
Hang your clothes on a hickory limb
But don't go near the water.

I sits with my toes in the brook,
And if anyone asks me for why,
I gives him a tap with my crook,
Necessity drives me, says I.

My Mother Said

My mother said that I never should
Play with the gipsies in the wood.
If I did, she would say,
Naughty girl to disobey,
Disobey, disobey,
Naughty girl to disobey.

I have a bonnet trimmed with blue.
Why don't you wear it? So I do.
When do you wear it? When I can,
Walking to church with my young man.

My young man has gone to France
To teach the ladies how to dance.
When he comes back he'll marry me,
Give me kisses, One, Two, Three.

Marry you! No such thing!
Yes, indeed, he bought me a ring;
Bought me a biscuit, bought me a tart.
What do you think of my sweetheart?

When I was Young

When I was young I used to go
With my daddy's dinner-o,
Baked potatoes, beef and steak,
Two red herrings, and a ha'penny cake;
I came to a river
And I couldn't get across,
I paid two pound
For an old dun horse,
Jumped on its back,
Its bones gave a crack;
I played upon my fiddle
Till the boat came back.

Tell Me When the Wedding Be

TO THE LADYBIRD

Bless you, bless you, burnie-bee,
Tell me when my wedding be;
If it be tomorrow day,
Take your wings and fly away.
Fly to the east, fly to the west,
Fly to him I love the best.

Brave news is come to town,
Brave news is carried;
Brave news is come to town,
Polly Dawson's to be married.

You can tell the parson's wife,
You can tell the people,
You can buy the wedding-gown.
I will thread the needle.

On Saturday night shall be my care
To powder my locks and curl my hair;
On Sunday morning my love will come in,
When he will marry me with a gold ring.

Little Jack Dandersprat
   Is my best suitor,
He has got house and land,
   And a little pewter;
First a new porridge pot,
   Then a brass ladle;
And if a baby comes,
   Then a new cradle.

Oh, rare Harry Parry,
   When will you marry?
When apples and pears are ripe.
I'll come to your wedding
   Without any bidding,
And dance and sing all the night.

The Milkmaid's Fortune

Where are you going to, my pretty maid,
  With your red rosy cheeks and your golden
    hair?
I'm going a-milking, sir, she said,
  And it's dabbling in the dew that makes the
    milkmaids fair.

May I go with you, my pretty maid,
  With your red rosy cheeks and your golden
    hair?
You're kindly welcome, sir, she said,
  And it's dabbling in the dew that makes the
    milkmaids fair.

Pray, will you marry me, my pretty maid,
  With your red rosy cheeks and your golden
    hair?
Yes, if you please, kind sir, she said,
  And it's dabbling in the dew that makes the
    milkmaids fair.

What is your father, my pretty maid,
    With your red rosy cheeks and your golden
        hair?
My father's a farmer, sir, she said,
    And it's dabbling in the dew that makes the
        milkmaids fair.

What is your fortune, my pretty maid,
    With your red rosy cheeks and your golden
        hair?
My face is my fortune, sir, she said,
    And it's dabbling in the dew that makes the
        milkmaids fair.

Then I can't marry you, my pretty maid,
    With your red rosy cheeks and your golden
        hair.
Nobody asked you, sir, she said,
    And it's dabbling in the dew that makes the
        milkmaids fair.

Flowers and Seasons

Mary, Mary, quite contrary,
    How does your garden grow?
With silver bells and cockle shells,
    And pretty maids all in a row.

Spring is showery, flowery, bowery;
Summer: hoppy, croppy, poppy;
Autumn: slippy, drippy, nippy;
Winter: breezy, sneezy, freezy.

Buttercups and daisies,
    Oh what pretty flowers,
Coming in the springtime
    To tell of sunny hours.
While the trees are leafless,
    While the fields are bare,
Buttercups and daisies
    Spring up everywhere.

Daffy-down-dilly has now come to town
In a yellow petticoat and a green gown.

Dancy-diddlety-poppety-pin,
Have a new dress when summer comes in;
   When summer goes out,
    'Tis all worn out,
Dancy-diddlety-poppety-pin.

   In spring I look gay,
    Dressed in handsome array,
In summer more clothing I wear;
   When colder it grows,
    I fling off my clothes,
And in winter quite naked appear.

[A tree]

A dish full of all kinds of flowers,
You can't guess this riddle in two hours.

[Honey]

Magpies

Magpie, magpie, chatter and flee,
Turn up your tail, and good luck come to me.

I saw eight magpies in a tree,
Two for you and six for me:
One for sorrow, two for mirth,
Three for a wedding, four for a birth;
Five for England, six for France,
Seven for a fiddler, eight for a dance.

A pie sat on a pear tree,
A pie sat on a pear tree,
A pie sat on a pear tree,
    Heigh-ho! Heigh-ho! Heigh-ho!

And once so merrily hopped she,
And twice so merrily hopped she,
And thrice so merrily hopped she,
    Heigh-ho! Heigh-ho! Heigh-ho!

RIDDLE

As white as milk, as black as coal,
And jumps in the road like a new-shod foal.

Crows

There were two crows sat on a stone,
    Fal de ral, fal de ral,
One flew away and there was one,
    Fal de ral, fal de ral;
The other seeing his neighbour gone,
    Fal de ral, fal de ral,
He flew away and then there were none,
    Fal de ral, fal de ral.

On the first of March,
The crows begin to search;
By the first of April
They are sitting still;
By the first of May
They've all flown away,
Coming greedy back again
With October's wind and rain.

SCARECROW'S SONG

Pigeons and crows, take care of your toes,
Or I'll pick up my clackers,
And knock you down backards,
Shoo away! Shoo away! Shoo!

In a Shower of Rain —

It rains, it hails, it batters, it blows,
And I am wet through all my clothes,
    I prithee, love, let me in!

Alack, alack, the clouds are so black,
And my coat is so flimsy and thin,
If we further ride on the rain will come down,
And wet little Sam to the skin.

Rain, rain, go away,
This is mother's washing day;
Rain, rain, pour down,
Wash my mother's night-gown.

Doctor Foster went to Gloucester
In a shower of rain;
He stepped in a puddle,
Right up to his middle,
And never went there again.

The Fishes don't Complain

Fishie, fishie, in the brook,
Daddy catch him with a hook,
Mama fry him in a pan,
Baby eat him like a man.

One, two, three, four, five,
Once I caught a fish alive,
Why did you let it go?
Because it bit my finger so.

Six, seven, eight, nine, ten,
Shall we go to fish again?
Not today, some other time,
For I have broke my fishing line.

Little Tommy Tittlemouse
Lived in a little house;
He caught fishes
In other men's ditches.

Numbers

One, two, three, four,
Mary at the cottage door,
Five, six, seven, eight,
Eating cherries off a plate.

One old Oxford ox opening oysters.
Two toads totally tired trying to trot to Tisbury.
Three thick thumping tigers taking toast for tea.
Four finicky fishermen fishing for finny fish.
Five frippery Frenchmen foolishly fishing for frogs.
Six sportsmen shooting snipe.
Seven Severn salmon swallowing shrimps.
Eight eminent Englishmen eagerly examining Europe.
Nine nimble noblemen nibbling nectarines.
Ten tinkering tinkers tinkering ten tin tinder-boxes.
Eleven elephants elegantly equipped.
Twelve typographical topographers typically translating
  types.

One's none,
Two's some,
Three's many,
Four's a penny,
Five's a little hundred.

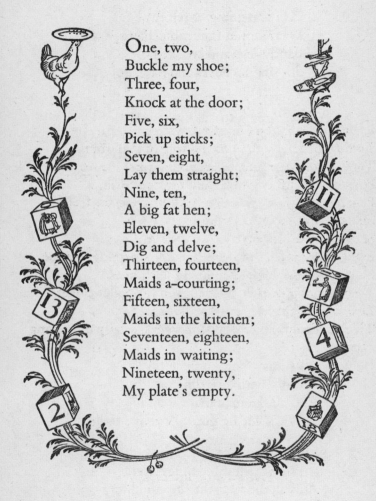

One, two,
Buckle my shoe;
Three, four,
Knock at the door;
Five, six,
Pick up sticks;
Seven, eight,
Lay them straight;
Nine, ten,
A big fat hen;
Eleven, twelve,
Dig and delve;
Thirteen, fourteen,
Maids a-courting;
Fifteen, sixteen,
Maids in the kitchen;
Seventeen, eighteen,
Maids in waiting;
Nineteen, twenty,
My plate's empty.

Meetings

As I was going to sell my eggs,
Who should I meet but Bandy-legs:
Bandy-legs and crooked toes,
Stir-about cheeks and a tea-pot nose.

As I was going to sell my butter,
Who should I meet but Stump-in-the-Gutter:
Stump-in-the-Gutter in a high collared cap,
Upon my word it made me laff!

As I was going up the hill,
    I met with Jack the piper;
And all the tune that he could play
    Was, 'Tie up your petticoats tighter.'

I tied them once, I tied them twice,
    I tied them three times over;
And all the song that he could sing
    Was, 'Carry me safe to Dover.'

As I was going up Pippen Hill,
  Pippen Hill was dirty.
There I met a pretty miss,
  And she dropped me a curtsy.

Little miss, pretty miss,
  Blessings light upon you!
If I had half a crown a day,
  I'd spend it all upon you.

One misty moisty morning,
When cloudy was the weather,
There I met an old man
Clothed all in leather;
Clothed all in leather,
With cap under his chin,
How do you do, and how do you do,
And how do you do again?

Tom, the Playful Piper

Tom he was a piper's son,
He learned to play when he was young,
But all the tunes that he could play
Was 'Over the hills and far away'.
    Over the hills and a great way off,
    The wind shall blow my top-knot off.

Tom with his pipe made such a noise,
That he pleased both the girls and boys;
They all danced while he did play
'Over the hills and far away'.
    Over the hills and a great way off,
    The wind shall blow my top-knot off.

Tom with his pipe did play with such skill
That those who heard him could never keep still;
Whenever he played they began for to dance,
Even pigs on their hind legs would after him prance.
    Over the hills and a great way off,
    The wind shall blow my top-knot off.

As Dolly was milking her cow one day,
Tom took out his pipe and began to play;
So Doll and the cow danced 'The Cheshire Round',
Till the pail was broken and the milk ran on the
    ground.
  Over the hills and a great way off,
  The wind shall blow my top-knot off.

He met old Dame Trot with a basket of eggs,
He used his pipe and she used her legs;
She danced about till the eggs were all broke,
She began for to fret, but he laughed at the joke.
  Over the hills and a great way off,
  The wind shall blow my top-knot off.

Tom saw a cross fellow was beating an ass,
Heavy laden with pots, pans, dishes, and glass;
He took out his pipe and he played them a tune,
And the poor donkey's load was lightened full soon.
  Over the hills and a great way off,
  The wind shall blow my top-knot off.

Peter Piper picked a peck of pickled pepper;
Did Peter Piper pick a peck of pickled pepper?
If Peter Piper picked a peck of pickled pepper,
Where's the peck of pickled pepper Peter Piper picked?

Careful Katie cooked a crisp and crinkly cabbage;
Did careful Katie cook a crisp and crinkly cabbage?
If careful Katie cooked a crisp and crinkly cabbage,
Where's the crisp and crinkly cabbage careful Katie
   cooked?

She sells sea-shells on the sea shore;
The shells that she sells are sea-shells I'm sure.
So if she sells sea-shells on the sea shore,
I'm sure that the shells are sea-shore shells.

A twister of twists once twisted a twist,
The twist that he twisted was a three-twisted twist;
If in twisting the twist, one twist should untwist,
The untwisted twist would untwist the twist.

Say These Twisters I Have Sung

Betty Botter bought some butter,
But, she said, this butter's bitter;
If I put it in my batter,
It will make my batter bitter,
But a bit of better butter
Will make my batter better.
So she bought a bit of butter
Better than her bitter butter,
And she put it in her batter,
And it made her batter better,
So 'twas better Betty Botter
Bought a bit of better butter.

There was a man, his name was Dob,
He had a wife, her name was Mob,
He had a dog, and called it Cob,
She had a cat called Chitterabob.
Cob, says Dob. Chitterabob, says Mob.
Cob was Dob's dog, Chitterabob Mob's cat.

Crooked Men

There was a crooked man,
  And he walked a crooked mile,
He found a crooked sixpence
  Against a crooked stile;
He bought a crooked cat,
  Which caught a crooked mouse,
And they all lived together
  In a little crooked house.

Peter White
Will ne'er go right;
Would you know the reason why?
He follows his nose
Wherever he goes,
And that stands all awry.

Crafty Men

There was a man in our town,
  And he was wondrous wise,
He jumped into a bramble bush
  And scratched out both his eyes.
And when he saw his eyes were out,
  With all his might and main
He jumped into another bush
  And scratched them in again.

There was a man and he had nought,
  And robbers came to rob him;
He crept up to the chimney top,
  And then they thought they had him.
But he got down on the other side,
  And then they could not find him;
He ran fourteen miles in fifteen days,
  And never looked behind him.

A Get-together of Gossips

It costs little Gossip her income for shoes,
To travel about and carry the news.

How do you do, neighbour?
Good neighbour, how do you do?
Very well, I thank you,
And how is Cousin Sue?
Cousin Sue is very well,
And sends her love to you,
And so does Cousin Bell.
Ah, how, pray, does she do?

Fire! Fire! said Mrs Dyer;
Where? Where? said Mrs Dare;
Up the town, said Mrs Brown;
Any damage? said Mrs Gamage;
None at all, said Mrs Hall.

Mrs Mason broke a basin,
Mrs Mack heard it crack,
Mrs Frost asked how much it cost,
Mrs Brown said half-a-crown,
Mrs Flory said what a story.

Miss One, Two, Three, could never agree,
As they gossiped around the tea-caddy.

I went to Noke,
But nobody spoke;
I went to Thame,
It was just the same;
Burford and Brill
Were silent and still;
But I went to Beckley,
And they spoke directly.

175

Soldier, Soldier, Will You Marry Me?

Oh, soldier, soldier, will you marry me,
    With your musket, fife, and drum?
Oh no, pretty maid, I cannot marry you,
    For I have no coat to put on.

Then away she went to the tailor's shop
    As fast as legs could run,
And bought him one of the very very best,
    And the soldier put it on.

Oh, soldier, soldier, will you marry me,
    With your musket, fife, and drum?
Oh no, pretty maid, I cannot marry you,
    For I have no shoes to put on.

Then away she went to the cobbler's shop
    As fast as legs could run,
And bought him a pair of the very very best,
    And the soldier put them on.

Oh, soldier, soldier, will you marry me,
　With your musket, fife, and drum?
Oh no, pretty maid, I cannot marry you,
　For I have no socks to put on.

Then away she went to the sock-maker's shop
　As fast as legs could run,
And bought him a pair of the very very best,
　And the soldier put them on.

Oh, soldier, soldier, will you marry me,
　With your musket, fife, and drum?
Oh no, pretty maid, I cannot marry you,
　For I have no hat to put on.

Then away she went to the hatter's shop
　As fast as legs could run,
And bought him one of the very very best,
　And the soldier put it on.

Oh, soldier, soldier, will you marry me,
　With your musket, fife, and drum?
Oh no, pretty maid, I cannot marry you,
　For I have a wife at home.

Blow, Wind, Blow

Blow, wind, blow! and go, mill, go!
That the miller may grind his corn;
   That the baker may take it,
   And into bread make it,
And bring us a loaf in the morn.

The north wind doth blow,
And we shall have snow,
And what will poor robin do then, poor thing?
   He'll sit in a barn,
   And keep himself warm,
And hide his head under his wing, poor thing.

   I went to the town
   And who went with me?
   I went up and down
   But nobody could see.

[Answer: The oldest whistler in the world.]

My lady Wind, my lady Wind,
Went round the house to find
  A chink to set her foot in;
She tried the key-hole in the door,
She tried the crevice in the floor,
  And drove the chimney soot in.

Arthur O'Bower has broken his band,
He comes roaring up the land;
The King of Scots, with all his power,
Cannot stop Arthur of the Bower.

  At Brill on the hill
  The wind blows shrill,
  The cook no meat can dress;
  At Stow-on-the-Wold
  The wind blows cold,
  I know no more than this.

Quirklums

As I went up the humber jumber,
    humber jumber, jeenio,
There I met Sir Hoker Poker
Carrying away campeenio.
If I'd had my tit-my-tat, my tit-my-tat,
    my teenio,
I'd never have let Sir Hoker Poker
Carry away campeenio.

As I went up a slippery gap
I met my Uncle Davy;
With timber toes and iron nose
Upon my word he would frighten the crows.

As I was going o'er Tipple Tine,
I met a flock of bonny swine;
    Some yellow necked,
    Some yellow backed,
They were the very bonniest swine
That ever went over Tipple Tine.

As I was going to St Ives,
I met a man with seven wives,
Each wife had seven sacks,
Each sack had seven cats,
Each cat had seven kits:
Kits, cats, sacks, and wives,
How many were there going to St Ives?

[The only one going to St Ives was myself.]

As I went over Lincoln Bridge,
I met Mister Rusticap;
Pins and needles on his back,
A-going to Thorney fair.

A Basket of Eggs

As I was walking in a field of wheat,
I picked up something good to eat;
Neither fish, flesh, fowl, nor bone,
I kept it till it ran alone.

As white as milk,
As soft as silk,
As yellow as gall,
As round as a ball;
Found by a baby,
Bought by a king,
Tell me this riddle
I'll give you a ring.

In marble halls as white as milk,
Lined with a skin as soft as silk,
Within a fountain crystal-clear,
A golden apple doth appear.
No doors there are to this stronghold,
Yet thieves break in and steal the gold.

Hickety, pickety, my black hen,
She lays eggs for gentlemen;
Gentlemen come every day,
To see what my black hen doth lay.
Some days five and some days ten,
She lays eggs for gentlemen.

There was an old man who lived in Middle Row,
He had five hens and a name for them, oh!
    Bill and Ned and Battock,
    Cut-her-foot and Pattock,
    Chuck, my lady Pattock,
    Go to thy nest and lay.

The Twelve Days of Christmas

The first day of Christmas my true love sent
   to me:
A partridge in a pear tree.

The second day of Christmas my true love sent
   to me:
Two turtle doves, and a partridge in a pear tree.

The third day of Christmas my true love sent
   to me:
Three French hens, two turtle doves, and a
   partridge in a pear tree.

The fourth day of Christmas my true love sent
   to me:
Four colly birds, three French hens, two turtle
   doves, and a partridge in a pear tree.

The fifth day of Christmas my true love sent
to me:
Five gold rings, four colly birds, three French
hens, two turtle doves, and a partridge in
a pear tree.

The sixth day of Christmas my true love sent
to me:
Six geese a-laying, five gold rings, four colly
birds, three French hens, two turtle doves,
and a partridge in a pear tree.

The seventh day of Christmas my true love sent
to me:
Seven swans a-swimming, six geese a-laying, five
gold rings, four colly birds, three French hens,
two turtle doves, and a partridge in a pear
tree.

The eighth day of Christmas my true love sent
  to me:
Eight maids a-milking, seven swans a-swimming,
  six geese a-laying, five gold rings, four
  colly birds, three French hens, two turtle
  doves, and a partridge in a pear tree.

The ninth day of Christmas my true love sent
  to me:
Nine drummers drumming, eight maids a-milking,
  seven swans a-swimming, six geese a-laying, five
  gold rings, four colly birds, three French hens, two
  turtle doves, and a partridge in a pear tree.

The tenth day of Christmas my true love sent
  to me:
Ten pipers piping, nine drummers drumming, eight
  maids a-milking, seven swans a-swimming, six
  geese a-laying, five gold rings, four colly birds,
  three French hens, two turtle doves, and a
  partridge in a pear tree.

The eleventh day of Christmas my true love sent
  to me:
Eleven ladies dancing, ten pipers piping, nine
  drummers drumming, eight maids a-milking, seven
  swans a-swimming, six geese a-laying, five gold
  rings, four colly birds, three French hens, two
  turtle doves, and a partridge in a pear tree.

The twelfth day of Christmas my true love sent
   to me:
Twelve lords a-leaping, eleven ladies dancing,
   ten pipers piping, nine drummers drumming, eight
   maids a-milking, seven swans a-swimming, six
   geese a-laying, five gold rings, four colly birds,
   three French hens, two turtle doves, and a
   partridge in a pear tree.

Incidentally

Page 14. *Hey diddle diddle* will be seen to make no more sense, and no less, when, as is fashionable with nursery classics, it is turned into Latin:

> Hei didulum! atque iterum didulum! Felisque Fidesque!
> Vacca super Lunae cornua prosiluit:
> Nescio qua Catulus risit dulcedine ludi;
> Abstulit et mira Lanx Cochleare fuga.

Nor does it make more sense in Russian. But it is nice to think that a rhyme that amazes English and American children has been translated, and also pleases young Russians. In fact, English nursery rhymes *en masse* seem to appeal to the children of Russia. Colourfully illustrated collections have been published in Moscow, and translations have been made by poets as eminent as Samuel Marshak and Korney Chukovsky.

Page 15. *Three wise men of Gotham.* Many countries have a village or district whose inhabitants are proverbial for a kind of wisdom which differs from that of their neighbours. England boasts several such places. There is Coggeshall in Essex, where the men are reputed to have pulled down one of their two windmills because there was not enough wind for both; and Haddenham in Buckinghamshire, where they build roofs on the walls to keep the ducks dry; and the Marlborough Downs where, notoriously, Wiltshire rustics, seeing the moon in a pond, attempted to rake it out.

For more than five hundred years, however, the merriest tales have been told about Gotham, where the villagers built a fence round the cuckoo so that they might keep her, and have summer all the year. Yet the traveller who arrives at this Nottinghamshire village and inquires, 'Is this the Gotham where the fools come from?' must be prepared for the reply, 'No, sir, this is the Gotham that the fools come to.'

Page 22. *There was a little man*. In 1893 this rhyme went through the Carrollian mind-mangle, and the first four lines became:

In stature the Manlet was dwarfish –
 No burly big Blunderbore he:
And he wearily gazed on the crawfish
 His Wifelet had dressed for his tea.
'Now reach me, sweet Atom, my gunlet,
 And hurl the old shoelet for luck:
Let me hie to the bank of the runlet,
 And shoot thee a Duck!'

She has reached him his minikin gunlet:
 She has hurled the old shoelet for luck:
She is busily baking a bunlet,
 To welcome him home with his Duck.
On he speeds, never wasting a wordlet,
 Though thoughtlets cling, closely as wax,
To the spot where the beautiful birdlet
 So quietly quacks.

Pages 23–5. *The House that Jack Built*. When in 1861 Edward Blanchard supplied Drury Lane Theatre with its annual Christmas pantomime, as he did for thirty-seven years, he called it *Harlequin and the House that Jack built*, and he included 'a poetic paraphrase of the ancient nursery legend, for the use of the rising generation, who might consider the simplicity of the original beneath them'. It began:

Behold the mansion swift upreared for Jack!
See the malt stored in many an ample sack.
Mark how the rat's felonious fangs invade
The golden stores in John's pavilion laid.
See how, with velvet foot and noiseless strides,
Subtle grimalkin to his quarry glides;
Grimalkin grim, that slew the fierce rodent
Whose tooth insidious Johann's sackcloth rent.

Lo! now the deep-mouthed canine foe's assault,
That vexed the avenger of the stolen malt,
Stored in the hallowed precincts of that hall,
That rose complete at Jack's creative call.

Page 29. *Here's to thee, good apple tree.* In the cider counties of the west, some farmers and their families have long maintained the custom of wassailing their apple trees on Twelfth Night. After supper they march into their orchards, carrying cider and hot cakes, tin trays, shotguns, and lanterns. They pour the cider on the roots of the biggest and best-bearing tree, they place the warm cake in a fork of the tree (some say for the robins), they chant in chorus, calling on the tree to be fruitful in its season, they beat on the tin trays, and the men shoot off their guns into the bare winter branches, which in eight months' time they pray will be heavy with apples – hats full, caps full, sacks full, and more fruit still for a pile beneath the stairs.

Page 30. *When the white pinks begin to appear.* In the calendar of old sayings there are several reminders that sheep should not be shorn too early in the year. 'Farmer, you may shear your sheep when the elder blossoms peep.' 'Shear your sheep in May and you'll shear them all away.' Similar counsel is, of course, prevalent respecting human apparel – 'Cast ne'er a clout till May be out.'

> Said the wise man unto his son,
> Keep on thy coat till May is done.
> If you would the doctor pay,
> Leave your flannels off in May.

Page 31. *Little Boy Blue come blow your horn* is a souvenir of the days of open fields, before the English countryside became a network of hedges, ditches, walls, and fences. The sheep and cows out at pasture readily strayed among the crops if their keepers fell asleep, or began singing together and did not keep a watchful eye on them. Thus Dorothy Osborne, in a letter to her future husband, describes her country life in Bedfordshire in May 1653:

The heat of the day is spent in reading or working, and about six or seven o'clock I walk out into a common that lies hard by the house, where a great many young wenches keep sheep and cows, and sit in the shade singing of ballads. . . . I talk to them, and find they want nothing to make them the happiest people in the world but the knowledge that they are so. Most commonly, when we are in the midst of our discourse, one looks about her, and spies her cows going into the corn, and then away they all run as if they had wings at their heels.

The frequency with which animals strayed in former times is also reflected, perhaps, in 'Little Bo-peep has lost her sheep'.

Page 31. *Pick, crow, pick, and have no fear*. In times past a further chore on the farm was scaring the birds from the new-sown crops. An army of little boys, equipped with rattles, clappers, whistles, and shrill voices, were stationed around the fields in this lonely pursuit. One of them was William Cobbett, who claimed that he could not remember the time when he did not earn his own living. 'My first occupation was driving the small birds from the turnip-seed, and the rooks from the pease. When I first trudged a-field, with my wooden bottle and my satchel slung over my shoulders, I was hardly able to climb the gates and stiles; and at the close of the day, to reach home was a task of infinite difficulty.' The 'crowboys' had special songs, often impudent, of which 'Pick, crow, pick' is a genuine example, recorded more than a century ago. It was also the recollection of a writer in *The East Anglian Magazine* (1961), who said he remembered it from his youth when there was a crowboy employed at Hemsby in Norfolk. One day the farmer on his rounds came unnoticed upon the lad, sitting up in a large oak tree, and these were the words he was happily singing.

Another bird-scarer's song, more ominous for the birds, appears on page 161.

Page 33. *Up a hill hurry me not*. This 'Speech of the Horse that Spoke to his Master' is centuries old; and in Black Beauty's day, or not long after, the rhyme was printed on broadsheets and distributed by animal-lovers to riders and drivers on the highway, with additions such as,

> With bit or rein O jerk me not,
> And when you are angry strike me not.

And this is how the horse should be shod, according to that 'fellow fine' John the Blacksmith:

> I put a bit upon the tae,
> To gar the horsie clim' the brae;
> Then a bit upon the sole,
> To help the horsie pay the toll;
> I put a bit upon the heel,
> To gar the horsie trot weel;
> And then a bit upon the brod.
> And there's a horsie weel shod.

Pages 36–40. *The Happy Courtship of Cock Robin and Jenny Wren.* Some versions are more flowery than ours, and more exact with their rhyme-words:

> 'Twas once upon a time
>   When Jenny Wren was young,
> So daintily she danced,
>   And so prettily she sung;
> Robin Redbreast lost his heart,
>   For he was a gallant bird;
> So he doffed his hat to Jenny Wren,
>   Requesting to be heard.

The rhyming of *said* with *bird* in our version can, we hope, be forgiven, since the words seem to come naturally, as they should do in traditional verse. Not that we think 'The Happy Courtship of Cock Robin' compares in antiquity with the 'Death and Burial of Cock Robin' (pp. 76–8). The two pieces are unlikely to belong to each other, and we have been careful to keep them separate. It is true that stanzas exist (printed as long ago as 1806) which purport to tell that the sparrow accidentally shot Cock

Robin at the wedding feast, but the verses are lame, and are almost certainly an interpolation.

Page 44. *A Friday night's dream.* Sir Thomas Overbury (1581–1613) held the character of a 'faire and happy Milkmaid' in such regard that he believed she feared no manner of ill when she was alone, for she was accompanied by old songs, honest thoughts, and prayers, if but short ones. And her dreams were so chaste that she dare tell them. 'Only a Fridaie's dreame is all her superstition: that she conceales for feare of anger.'

Here are two more dreams:

> Oh, were I King of France,
>   Or, better, Pope of Rome,
> I'd have no fighting men abroad,
>   No weeping maids at home.

> Oh, Jack will dance, and Polly will run,
> And baby will laugh to see the fun.
> If I had a carriage, and a sister beside,
> I'd take her dressed in her Sunday best
> Every day for a ride.

Pages 49–52. *London Bridge is Broken Down.* The verses given here are exactly as they are reported to have been 'plaintively warbled' more than two hundred years ago by an old lady who was born in the reign of Charles II, and who lived until nearly the end of the reign of George II. Almost certainly the song was already old in Charles II's time (see *The Oxford Dictionary of Nursery Rhymes*).

Pages 62–3. *Sing a Song of Sixpence.* The continuation on page 63 was sent us by Mrs Moira Newell, whose mother learnt it from her mother, who came from Ayrshire. Jenny Wren was also the heroine in the version Randolph Caldecott illustrated in 1880, but we have here the further information that the maid's nose was replaced, albeit imperfectly, with the aid of sealing wax. Lundyfoot was a brand of snuff which, so it is said, would make a man snort and snuffle if he took too much. It was named after Lundy Foot, a Dublin tobacconist, whose address is given in the *Dublin Directory*, 1776, as 8 Essex Bridge. We went to a London snuff shop hoping to buy some, but the proprietor had never heard of it.

Page 79. *Two pigeons flying high.* Who is ever tired of hearing the story of the figures on the willow-pattern plate? Long ago in old China there lived a wealthy mandarin whose ornate house, surrounded by outbuildings and large trees, may be seen to the right of the picture. This mandarin had an only daughter named Koong-see, who was as beautiful as the sunrise; and he had a clever young secretary named Chang, who had helped him to amass his wealth. Koong-see and Chang loved each other dearly; but they dared not tell the mandarin of their love because Chang was poor. They used to meet secretly in the evening in the grove of orange trees beside the house, and they would dream of the day when Chang, too, would be rich, and they could marry. The year of their fancy had only two seasons, spring-time and summer. But one day the mandarin learned of their meetings. Instantly he banished Chang from his estate. He built the wooden fence which crosses the footpath to his house. And he betrothed his daughter to a friend of his, a man as rich as he and almost as old, a Ta-jin, a duke of high degree.

To make sure that Koong-see would do as he wished he imprisoned her in the outbuilding by the water's edge, and he told her that her wedding to the Ta-jin would take place at the propitious phase of the moon when the peach tree bloomed in the spring. The willow tree, as may be seen, was already in flower, but the peach tree had scarcely yet formed its buds.

The weeks went by and sorrowfully Koong-see watched the buds swell on the peach tree, and the willow blossom seemed about to wither. Then one day, looking out of her window, she saw a coconut shell fitted with a little sail floating across the water. In it she found a message from Chang urging her to be of good courage, and to be ready to escape.

A little after this the Ta-jin paid a stately visit to Koong-see's father to make the final arrangements for the wedding. He was attended by a great concourse of soldiers and retainers, and brought with him a large box of precious jewels for Koong-see. Unnoticed in the throng of the Ta-jin's servants, young Chang slipped into the house. While the mandarin and the Ta-jin were feasting, Chang found Koong-see and they fled away together.

So it is that running across the bridge beside the willow tree may be seen, first, the lovely Koong-see holding her distaff; second, young Chang carrying the jewel box; and third, the mandarin, who had espied them, chasing them with a whip.

The rest of the story is also depicted on the willow-pattern plate. The young lovers were too fleet of foot for the mandarin, and they managed to hide in the gardener's cottage on the other side of the bridge. When the Ta-jin heard what had happened his rage was such that he frothed at the mouth. He vowed that both the lovers should die, and ordered his soldiers to search every house in every village for miles around. Fortunately, when the soldiers came to the gardener's cottage, Koong-see and Chang were able to jump out of a window into a boat; and the boat in which they sailed hundreds of miles away down the river is nevertheless clearly visible. So, too, is the distant island in the mighty river where Koong-see and Chang landed, and where they married, and where Chang wrote books and prospered, and built Koong-see a fine house. Indeed, Chang became so learned his fame spread through China, and eventually it reached the ears of the Ta-jin, whose passion for revenge had never abated. He ordered his soldiers to sail down the great river and attack the island, and the two lovers died defending their home. Then, says the legend, Koong-see and her lover were transformed into two immortal doves, flying high for all to see, emblems of the un-dying love that two people can have for each other.

Page 80. *If I had gold in goupins.* 'If I had gold in handfuls.' Indeed, to be precise, 'If I had gold in double handfuls', for a goupin or gowpen (Old Norse *gaupn*) usually meant as much as could be held in the bowl formed by both hands placed together. In Scotland a lock or gowpen of meal was sometimes the perquisite of the miller's servant.

Page 87. *There was an old woman who lived under a hill.* As an eighteenth-century commentator remarked, '*She lived under the hill, and if she's not gone she lives there still.* Nobody will presume to contradict this.'

Pages 88–9. *Robin-a-Thrush.* This Suffolk version is from the singing of a nurse towards the end of the eighteenth century, and is taken from Broadwood and Maitland's *English County Songs*, 1893, by courtesy of J. B. Cramer & Co. Ltd.

Page 90. *They that wash on Monday have all the week to dry.* 'My poor old Granny would turn in her grave if she could see the lines of washin' hanging out everywheres on a Sunday,' said Mrs Paddick.

'I suppose if a woman's out at work all the week, Sunday is the only day she can do her washing, Mrs Paddick.'

'But women always did goo out to work, mum. My mother went turnip hoein' an' hay-makin' an' what-all. An' there was ten of we. They weren't so unaccountable lapsy in them days, as they got up earlier of a Monday mornin' an' got the washin' done afore breakfast. Many a time I've hear mother sayin' that old rhyme, as I was learnin' little Mavis to say on'y the other day.'

'Isn't there anything about washing on Sunday, Mrs Paddick?' asked *The West Sussex Gazette's* correspondent, who writes under the name 'A Sussex Woman'.

'No, mum,' Mrs Paddick replied, 'on account of nobody ever thought of doin' such a unaccountable wicked thing.'

Page 103. *Jack and Jill.*

> Then up Jack got, and home did trot,
>   As fast as he could caper,
> To old Dame Dob, who plastered his nob
>   With vinegar and brown paper.

Alison Uttley in her book *Country Things* tells how, when she was a child, the ploughboy's remedy for toothache or headache was an application of vinegar and brown paper. A thick piece of brown paper was heated by the fire and dipped in a saucer of vinegar. It was sprinkled with pepper and bound on the head with a woollen scarf.

And here, in more exalted style, is a riddle generally attributed to Bishop Wilberforce:

> 'Twas not on Alpine snow and ice,
>   But homely English ground,
> 'Excelsior!' was their device,
>   But sad the fate they found.
> They did not climb for love of fame,
>   They followed duty's call.
> They were united in their aim,
>   But parted in their fall.

Page 103. *Goosey, goosey gander* is a nursery rhyme which seems to us unsatisfactory, being neither evocative nor melodious; and it is, we suspect, a hybrid. As late as 1896, in *The Warwickshire Word-Book*, the first four lines were given on their own as a nursery rhyme; and the four following lines appeared in another part of the glossary as a Midlands folk-rhyme addressed to the cranefly, 'Daddy-long-legs', or 'Harry-long-legs':

> 'Arry, 'Arry-lung-legs,
> Couldn't say 'is pray'rs,
> Ketch 'im by the left leg,
> An' throw 'im down stairs.

Pages 106–7. *I saw a peacock with a fiery tail*, etc. These three rhymes stand as a poetic warning of the embarrassments and embranglements awaiting those who neglect their punctuation – as Peter Quince found with his Prologue, and as Ralph Roister Doister learned to his dumbfusion, four centuries ago, when his love-letter to Dame Custance was read out:

Sweet mistress whereas I love you nothing at all
Regarding your substance and riches chief of all
For your personage beauty demeanor and wit
I commend me unto you never a whit
Sorry to hear report of your good welfare
For as I hear say such your conditions are
That ye be worthy favour of no living man
To be abhorred of every honest man
To be taken for a woman inclined to vice
Nothing at all to virtue giving her due price.

Page 114. *Girls and boys come out to play.* Are the girls and boys being summoned to a boisterous night-game of Kick the Can, or Tally-ho Dogs, or Jacky Shine a Light, such as children join in today under the street lamps? Or is this, perhaps, a beyond-experience and long-ago invitation from the light-bodied folk, and she who becomes queen – in this nineteenth-century record-ing of the rhyme – shall she become Queen of the Fairies?

Fairy-folk scarcely show their faces in the land of nursery rhyme, so perhaps this fairy idea is just a fancy. Even so, there is no harm in recalling the fairies' song in *The Maydes Metamor-phosis*, a play printed in 1600 that 'hath beene sundrie times Acted by the Children of Powles':

> By the moone we sport and play,
> With the night begins our day;
> As we daunce, the deaw doth fall;
> Trip it little urchins all.

Ring-a-ring o' roses. There are still some different verses for this game in different parts of Britain. The first verse is the one usually sung; the second is known in parts of the West Country; and the third is from a young girl on the Scottish Border; while in Glasgow little children (and their mothers) continue to hold out against English radio and rhyme books, and sing:

> Ring-a-ring a roses,
> A cappie cappie shell,
> The dog's awa to Hamilton,
> To buy the wean a bell.

The wean'll no tak' it,
I'll tak' it tae mysel',
Ring-a-ring a roses,
A cappie cappie shell.

Page 117. *The Recruiting Sergeant.* We have had this song from two sources. We found it in a junk shop, printed on a piece of sheet music designated 'for little singers' and watermarked 1825; and we were sent an oral version by Mrs Susan Todd of Long Sutton, whose grandmother's Derbyshire nurse used to sing it a hundred years ago, beating time with her forefingers on the brass rail of the nursery fireguard. Was it, perhaps, the sergeant's music that kept Johnny so long at the fair?

Page 124. *This little pig went to market.* In Somerset it is traditional to say 'This choogey pig went to market, this choogey pig stayed at home'; and in the West Riding they say:

This little pig went to market,
This little pig stopped at hooam,
This little pig gate a butter-cake,
This little pig gate nooan
But this little pig said, Nip a bit,
nip a bit, afoor it's all done!

Pages 126–30. *The Queen of Hearts and the Stolen Tarts.* This story comes from *Mother Hubbard and Other Old Friends*, by Brother Sunshine, one of the most gorgeously old-fashioned of the three hundred nursery-rhyme books in our collection. Produced about 1860, when publishers could afford to have a large illustration on each page and have each illustration water-coloured by hand, there is no stinting of rosy cheeks, royal blue dresses, yellow thrones, and curtains which are purple in one picture, and best bottle-green in the next. Pauline Baynes has admirably reproduced the melodrama of the original illustrations. The text needed some furbishing here and there.

Page 131. *Nick-Nock, Padlock.* This is the oldest copy of the verses we know, and the most delightful, of a song that has recently come back into popularity. It was collected in 1916 by the veteran scholar Dr Margaret Murray, who learnt the verses from an old servant, a native of Luton, who had heard them sung in that town when a child, by a very old woman. Dr Murray, writing with customary alertness in her ninety-ninth year, enjoined us to observe that in the refrain the word was TRODDLING. 'I made certain at the time that the word had an R in it.'

Page 135. *When I was a lad as big as my Dad.* Versions of this rhyme are particularly popular in the North Country, and this is one of several that Northerner II has printed in his column in the *Yorkshire Post.* 'From the ignition of the bale of cotton,' a Helmsley correspondent told him, 'the speed of reciting increases. My father still amuses his grandchildren with it, and I have heard him say it as many as six times before his listeners were satisfied.'

Pages 138–9. *The Frog and the Crow.* The words, to a merry tune, have long been traditional in the family of Mrs E. Lucia Turnbull, the children's author, who kindly set them down for us; and we give her version (in which verse 3 in notably superior) rather than the one usually printed, which Walter Crane included in *The Baby's Opera.*

The song appears to be at least three hundred years old. Mr Martin Hamlyn of Peter Murray Hill Ltd, the antiquarian booksellers, has shown us a manuscript commonplace book of the early seventeenth century, in which appear three embryonic verses of 'The Crow & the Frogge', beginning:

There Was a craftie greate Crowe flew ouer a pande.

Page 140. *Pussy at the fireside.* In Scotland:

Jock in the kail pot up tae the knees,
Baby in the cradle playin' wi' the keys,
Pussy at the fireside, suppin' up her brose,
Doon fell a cinder and burned pussy's nose.

Pages 148–9. *The Long Way to Wealth* comes from Sowerby Bridge, near Halifax. To lope or loup is to leap, and 'Footit and

Half', which the calf played, is a leap-frog game in which the boy appointed 'Footit and Half' decides how difficult the next jump shall be, but he must be able to do it himself.

The words were collected many years ago by Mr H. W. Harwood, who is a walking anthology of West Riding verse. Another of his ditties about unappreciated legacies goes:

> Me father died a year ago
> An' left me all 'is riches;
> A wooden leg an' a feather bed
> An' a pair o' leather britches.
> A teeah pot without a knob,
> A cup without a handle,
> A 'bacca box without a lid
> An' a 'ofe a farding candle.

Page 150. *If all the seas were one sea, what a great sea it would be.* And if a parent were to introduce this rhyme at bath-time, what a lot of extra mopping-up of bath water there would be.

Page 151. *I sits with my toes in the brook.* This epigram by Horace Walpole has twice been sent us as a traditional nursery rhyme, so a nursery rhyme it shall be. It reminds us of Peter Prim in *Original Ditties for the Nursery*, published in the year of Trafalgar:

> Peter Prim! Peter Prim!
> Why do you in stockings swim?
> Peter Prim gave this reply,
> To make such fools as you ask why!

Page 154. *To the Ladybird.* In such manner Gay's love-sick Hobnelia cast her spell:

> This Lady-fly I take from off the grass,
> Whose spotted back might scarlet red surpass.
> *Fly*, Lady-Bird, *North, South, or East, or West,*
> *Fly where the Man is found that I love best.*
> He leaves my hand, see to the West he's flown,
> To call my true-love from the faithless town.

Page 158. *Spring is showery, flowery, bowery.* Anybody can be forgiven for wanting to adjust these adjectives according to their own experience of each month. Richard Brinsley Sheridan's reckoning was: January snowy, February flowy, March blowy; April show'ry, May flow'ry, June bow'ry; July moppy, August croppy, September poppy; October breezy, November wheezy, December freezy.

Page 162. *It rains, it hails.* 'Here is a vile day,' wrote Sir Walter Scott in his Journal for 21 April 1827. ' – downright rain, which disconcerts an inroad of bairns from Gattonside, and, of course, annihilates a part of the stock of human happiness. But what says the proverb of your true rainy day –

> 'Tis good for book, 'tis good for work,
> For cup and can, or knife and fork.'

Yet had the day brought snow instead of rain each child would have been merry, and taken up the gleeful cry:

> The folk in the east
> Are pluckin' their geese,
> And sendin' their feathers
> tae oor toon.

Page 164. *One old Oxford ox.* This piece of numerical nonsense was popular a hundred years ago for a fireside game. One of the company would begin by intoning the first line, 'One old Oxford ox opening oysters', and the others in turn repeated the words. Then the first player added a line, 'One old Oxford ox opening oysters; two toads totally tired trying to trot to Tisbury', and each person had to repeat these two lines, and then three lines together, and then four, an extra line being added at each round. Any player who laughed or who made a mistake had to pay a forfeit, which could later be redeemed only by the performance of some difficult or delicate exercise such as reciting the names of the Kings of England, or bowing to the wittiest person present, kneeling to the prettiest, and kissing 'the one you love the best'.

Pages 174–5. *A Get-together of Gossips.* Let little jabberboxes, chinwaggers, chattermongers, babblemerchants, and other unpaid jawsmiths take heed:

> If you your lips would keep from slips
>   Five things observe with care;
> To whom you speak, of whom you speak,
>   And how, and when, and where.

Small thanks may currently be the market price for such advice, but the grandmothers of yesteryear added a further caution:

> If you your ears would keep from jeers,
>   These things keep meekly hid:
> Myself and me, and my and mine,
>   And how I do and did.

And more than this we are not prepared to say.

Index of Principal Subjects
of the Rhymes

Index of First Lines

215

Shall we tell a last tale
About a snail?
It jumped in the fire and burnt its tail.
Shall we tell a last tale
About a tub?
The bottom's out or else we would.

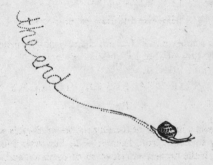

Also in the Young Puffin format

THE YOUNG PUFFIN BOOK OF VERSE
ed. Barbara Ireson

A deluge of poems about such fascinating subjects as birds and balloons, mice and moonshine, farmers and frogs, pigeons and pirates, especially chosen to please young people of four to eight.

MICE AND MENDELSON
Joan Aiken

A new collection of stories set in Midnight Park, featuring an old Orkney pony (Mr Mendelson) and two mice, Bertha and Gertrude, who give piano recitals for him each evening.

THE LITTLE GIRL AND THE TINY DOLL
Aingelda and Edward Ardizzone

Abandoned in a supermarket freezer, the tiny doll is visited and cheered up by the little girl, until at last she can be rescued.

THE DWARFS OF NOSEGAY
Paul Biegel

There are at least a hundred of the tiny moorland dwarfs whose favourite food is honey squeezed from heather bells, but Peter Nosegay, smallest and youngest, is the bravest and cleverest of them all, and the kindest too.

CASEY THE UTTERLY IMPOSSIBLE HORSE
Anita Feagles

Mike finds a horse who wants to live in the garage, but it decides it wants to be called Mike too, or failing that, Kitty Cat. It's fun to have a horse, but the drawbacks are only too obvious!

THE GHOST ELEPHANT
Alan C. Jenkins

The story of an African village where the inhabitants believe they are being haunted by the ghost of an elephant they had hunted.

THE OLD NURSE'S STOCKING-BASKET
Eleanor Farjeon

'Children,' said the Old Nurse, 'stop quarrelling or you know what,' and the children always stopped quarrelling at once, for none of them wanted to miss the bedtime tales about the little princes and princesses, sea captains and peasants' sons and daughters she had known in hundreds and hundreds of years as a children's nurse.

THE SHRINKING OF TREEHORN
Florence Parry Heide

Treehorn knows very well that boys don't shrink, but he is fast vanishing under the table all the same, and it's no help that none of the grown-ups even notice his predicament!

DORRIE AND THE BIRTHDAY EGGS
DORRIE AND THE WIZARD'S SPELL
DORRIE AND THE HAUNTED HOUSE
DORRIE AND THE GOBLIN

Patricia Coombs

A series of delightful books about the little witch, Dorrie, her cat, Gink, and her mother The Big Witch. They all live cheerfully together in a house with a tower, and have many exciting adventures.

CHANGING OF THE GUARD and
WALLPAPER HOLIDAY

H. E. Todd

Two charming stories about the adventures of Timothy Trumper and his family. Ideal for reading aloud, and illustrated by Val Biro.

WORZEL GUMMIDGE AT THE FAIR

Keith Waterhouse and Willis Hall

Here he is again, the scatty scarecrow, neglecting his crow-scaring and trying to win back Aunt Sally from a fairground Strong Man.

MATTHEW'S SECRET SURPRISES

Teresa Verschoyle

Day-to-day stories about Matthew, who wears a different hat for every interesting experience in his new home in the country.

Who is he?

His name is Smudge, and he's the mascot of the Junior Puffin Club.

What is that?

It's a Club for children between 4 and 8 who are beginning to discover and enjoy books for themselves.

How does it work?

On joining, members are sent a Club badge and Membership Card, a sheet of stickers, and their first copy of the magazine, *The Egg*, which is sent to them four times a year. As well as stories, pictures, puzzles and things to make there are competitions to enter and, of course, news about new Puffins.

For details of cost and an application form, send a stamped addressed envelope to:

The Junior Puffin Club
Penguin Books Limited
Bath Road
Harmondsworth
Middlesex UB7 oDA